Dead Woman Creek

Buck Edwards

Dead Woman Creek is a work of fiction. Names, characters, places, and incidents either are the product of the author's imagination or are used fictitiously. Any resemblance to actual persons, living or dead, events, or locals is entirely coincidental.

Cover Design by Rachel Oline Boruff
RachelThorntonPhotography.com

First Edition

For:

My wife, Rebecca

Chapter 1

EVEN AS THE stranger entered the town he could see there was a dead man lying in the middle of the wide street. A crowd of men and boys were beginning to gather around the fallen man, their boots working up the red dust and causing devils to swirl underfoot. The stranger's horse was tired, and he was tired, and so he did not hurry but he could see, further down the street, another man standing alone against a rail, his long arm resting at his side and a pistol still being gripped in his hand.

He passed the crowd now and looked down at the dead man as he went—barely a man, more a boy—his legs twisted under him and the blue barrel of a rifle protruding from beneath his body. One of the townsfolk was kneeling, his open hand stroking the dead man's hair, as with affection. Then came a wail from the boardwalk as a young woman appeared through a door and instantly threw herself into their midst. Her cries increased and were sorrowful and like the dust they were carried off by the wind.

Looking away he let his eyes fall next on the other man, who must have been the shooter, who had not moved but only stared at the crowd with forced indifference. When the stranger's horse came alongside the shooter he pulled up. Another boy, it seemed, not more than nineteen or twenty, longish red sweat curls at the temple, a vest and chaps. He wore spurs and his shirtsleeves seemed too short for his long arms. His mustache was faint and unmanly.

He looked the kid over and then said, "You got a job?"

The kid eyed him. "What's it to you?"

"Cause I'm askin." His horse stood still, weary from a long day, a layer of dust in its mane. He turned away and sized up the town, its single street stretching out into openness, boardwalks of raw lumber on both sides, a single row of unpainted houses, a store, a door that looked to lead to a tiny saloon, a livery and several other nondescript buildings. "If you're done here you might holster that thing. I reckon there'll be hell to pay here in a minute."

"Let em try."

"I'll ask again. You ridin for somebody?"

The kid brought the pistol up slowly and poked its barrel around until it found its way into the holster. "Starkweather. I ride for Starkweather. Why you want to know?"

"Maybe I need a job. I might be lookin."

The kid stared at him, saw the gray whiskers, how they had gathered thick at his chin, and the scraggly swath across his weathered cheeks. "Kind of old for working cattle, ain't you?" There was youthful arrogance in his tone.

He leaned heavily against his saddle horn. "You just saw me ride in here, didn't you? If I can sit a horse I reckon I can punch a cow."

The kid smirked. "Starkweather ain't hiring."

There was noise behind him now. The wailing woman had been led away but now there were curses being shouted and boot heels on the boardwalk.

"This might be a good time to get back to your herd, cowboy."

"You sure are minding my business. I don't remember askin."

He looked close at the kid's eyes, trying to detect fear, then pulled the reins and turned his horse back up the street in the direction he had just come. "Suit yourself." But by the time he had plodded back to the crowd he could hear the groan of leather and the thunder of the cowboy's horse hightailing out of town.

Several of the townsfolk had pulled a door off a shop and were preparing to lay the body on it. One man, bespeckled and wearing a soiled apron, looked up at him. "You with him?" he asked angrily.

"I ain't with anybody."

"Why'd you let him get away? He done killed the Tundel boy. And now he's gone."

The stranger touched his beard. "He won't be hard to find. You got law here?"

One of the other men laughed venomously then spit on the ground.

The man with the apron straightened up, hands on his hips. "That about says it, mister. Now unless you got business here, I think you ought to keep riding."

Ignoring this, and without invitation he slung his leg over his saddle and stepped down from his horse. He took his hat off and beat the dust from his pants then returned it to his graying head. Then he stepped to the door upon which the dead man lay, and lifted one end of it. The man who had spit took up the other end and together they carried the deceased across the street and into the dry goods store where he was placed across a table.

Saying nothing he stepped back outside where he saw one of the youngsters had taken the reins of his horse and was tying it to the hitching rail. The boy looked up at him with an empty stare. His cheeks showed the tracks of grimy tears.

"Was he kin?" he asked, stepping to the boy.

The boy shook his head.

"But you knew him."

A nod.

"It's not a nice thing. To see someone killed like that."

The boy reached inside his pocket and retrieved a peppermint stick, his shoulders jerking slightly in an effort to fight off more tears.

The stranger knelt down so he was looking at the boy face to face. "Did he give you that?" He tipped his head in the direction of the store where the dead man lay.

The boy nodded again.

"You have a name?"

After a slow, difficult swallow, the boy said, "Tanner."

The stranger looked around, studying the town again. A few people had poked their heads out of their houses now, several more walked uncomfortably toward the store. A flatbed wagon was parked across the street. The two horses hitched to it were standing in nervous silence, their wide eyes startled and afraid. The woman's sobs could still be heard but only faintly. She was behind closed doors, somewhere, being comforted. Behind him, gazing back in the direction he had just come he could see in the far distance the ragged range of mountains and the first lacing of snow in the high places.

"Tanner."

The boy's eyes lifted.

"I reckon you ought to eat that candy. It's why he gave it to you. It would honor him."

There were other boys, older, standing at a distance, watching, so the stranger put his hand on Tanner's shoulder. "Is there a place this old hoss could get a drink? And maybe some oats?"

The boy pointed with the same hand that held the peppermint. "Pa's stable," he said.

"This critter's name is Hunter, and he's my best friend. Do you suppose you could walk him over to your pa's stable and get him a drink? He's gentle as a daisy."

A thin smile worked at Tanner's sad mouth.

"I'll come along in a bit and rub him down." He stood up and touching the saddle, patted Hunter on the neck, then pulled the Winchester from its sheath.

Tanner took the reins and led the horse away and the other boys scattered. Turning, the stranger stepped back up on the boardwalk and reentered the store. The man with the spectacles and apron had straightened the dead man's legs out and was now folding his arms across his chest. The other man—the spitting man—was shaking out a bed sheet and preparing to lay it over the corpse.

"You still here?" he said.

The stranger ignored him, speaking instead to the storekeeper. "This Tundel fellow. He live near here?"

"They all live here. About four miles out."

"All?"

The storekeeper nodded. "The old man and his boys. Four in all, counting the old man." He looked down at the dead man. "Well, there was four. Now there are three."

"Farmers?"

"You ask a lot of questions mister." It was the angry man again.

"Habit, I reckon."

"A bad habit, I'd say."

"Are you going out to fetch the bad news to his kin?" the stranger asked.

"No, I ain't."

The storekeeper spoke up. "Little George already set out. He'll break it easy. He's good about things like that."

"Who was the shooter? You know him?"

"Brady Quinn. Rides for Starkweather. Comes in by himself. Long running feud with Junson here." He placed his hand on the dead man's shoulder.

The stranger scratched his whiskery chin. "I'm looking for someone. But it ain't this Brady Quinn."

The angry man spoke up again. "I sure hope you ain't bringing any trouble to this town."

The storekeeper fidgeted, toying with his apron. "Clive. Can't you see? This here *is* trouble. We already got it. Them Tundels won't stand for this."

"Where's Starkweather's spread?" the stranger asked.

"There's a creek a ways out of town. East. Everything across that creek is his. Or so he likes to think." The storekeeper glanced at Clive then back to the stranger. "I don't mean no disrespect, mister, but this has been a very bad day for us. And I'm afraid it's going to get worse. Clive here might be right. Maybe it would be a friendly notion if you'd tell us who you are. There's lots of nervous folks in this town. And they just got more nervous."

The stranger straightened up. His hat cast a shadow across his face. He moved back to the corpse, the leather of his gun belt creaking. The ugly pistol was mostly hidden in the holster but the grip was of black walnut and seemed to wink a sinister black eye when he moved. He pulled the sheet back and stared at the young dead man's face. "A man ought not to die this way." His voice was barely a whisper. "Feller ought to be able to live out his life."

The storekeeper and Clive exchanged glances.

The stranger gently placed the sheet back over the dead man then turned and faced the two men.

"Name's Boone Crowe," he said. "United States Marshal. Wyoming Territory."

August Tundel was at the highest point of the farm with a shovel, opening up a ditch that allowed water from the stream to flow into the cornfield. It would be the last water before he and his brothers would traipse down through the rows, stripping the corn from the stalks. They'd fill their bags then dump them into the crib. Once the crib was pulled back down to the house, Ma and Lucy would pile it down into the cellar for winter food.

He watched where he had removed the dam and water coursed down through the turned soil and into the rows. After a while he straightened up and took in the full view of the farm—the old house with the runway connecting Virgil and Lucy's added rooms; the barn and corral; the small bunkhouse where he slept; and the garden where Ma was standing this very minute, pinning up some wash on the line. Beyond, on the opposite hill, grazed a dozen beeves and several horses. Tame ducks and chickens and white geese marched freely in the yard and tall grass.

Turning his gaze toward the horizon he saw a trail of dust coming off the next hill caused by a single rider heading this way. It couldn't be Junson, he thought, because Junson took the wagon. So he stood, shovel in hand, watching and waiting. In the meantime he pulled the kerchief from his neck and dipped it into the water and wiped it across his sweaty face, then retied it around his neck. He wondered if he should have brought his rifle up with him. There had been riders watching the place lately. Lone riders just sitting their horse at the top of a rise, their long dark shadows stretching out to their side like a man partnered with a demon. But this rider was still coming on and from here it looked like Little George.

"August," Little George panted when he finally reached the hilltop, as if it had been he and not his horse that'd carried them out there.

"I thought that was you. Looks like you worked up a lather getting here. What gives?"

Little George wore a face of worry. "Where's yer pa? He around?"

August Tundel turned and pointed over the farthest horizon. "Him and Virgil set out to Bradley. Won't be back till tomorrow."

Little George let his head fall in frustration. He pulled off his hat then put it back on again. "What about yer ma?"

"She's down yonder by the house. What's wrong, Little George? You look about half sick."

He looked at August and shook his head. "I *am* sick. Damn sick. It's yer brother."

August stiffened. "Junson?"

Little George got down off his horse, and then knelt all the way to the ground. He picked up a handful of dirt and gave it a toss. "Yer brother went and got himself kilt, August."

August felt his body jerk inward. He let go of the shovel handle and heard it thud to the ground. "No."

A sob came from Little George's throat. "Oh, Lord, August. I saw it. I saw it."

A chill plagued August's neck. "Was it a shootin?"

Little George nodded.

August walked over and touched Little George's horse along the neck. He was trying to think. He looked across the cornfield and down into the yard. His mother was still there. The clothes were hung on the line but she was standing there, hands on her hips, looking up at him. She'd seen the rider and was wondering who it was and what he wanted way out here.

"I thought yer pa would be here. I was going to tell him. But now you'll have to tell him."

Not hesitating August said, "I'll tell him. I'll have to tell Ma first. And Lucy."

"It was one of Starkweather's riders done it."

"Quinn?"

"That's him."

August put the toe of his boot into the soft dirt and kicked a clod away. He'd seen it coming. Pa should have taken Junson with him and sent Virgil into town. But what was that cowpuncher doing in Dry Branch anyway. Starkweather's punchers hung out in Garfield. Or Fort Tillman. They never bothered with Dry Branch.

"It was that girl, wasn't it," he said finally, looking at Little George.

Little George's shoulders sagged. "Appeared so."

August spit on the ground then wiped at his mouth. "Better tell me so I can tell Ma."

"Ain't much to tell. It happened real fast. Yer brother'd been in and out of the store a couple of times loadin supplies onto his wagon. It looked like he was fetchin to leave when the cowboy come ridin in like his horse was afire. He jumped down right there in the street and saw Junson crossin to the hotel. We was all busy. Amos was in his store. Mr. Leyland had just come out of his saloon. Junson stopped for a second and was talking to the little Hornfisher boy. Tanner. I was sweepin out the saloon. When Junson got to the middle of the street I heard the cowboy say something to him but I couldn't tell what it was. Yer brother was carrying his rifle at his side, but I swear I never saw it move. Next thing yer brother said something back and the cowboy drew and shot him dead. He was still holding the rifle when he fell."

August squared his shoulders. "Murder, then."

"I ain't sayin. It was too fast. And yer brother did…I mean, Junson was carrying a gun. His rifle. Hell, August. I don't know."

"What'd Quinn do then? After he'd done his killin?"

"He just stood there. He stood there for a long time. Like he was darin the whole rest of us to say a word."

"Is he still in town?"

Little George shook his head. "Some stranger rode in. They talked for a minute then the cowboy lit out."

"Who was the stranger?"

"Never saw him before. Older feller. That's when Mr. Leyland fetched me out here to tell you the bad news. I'm awful sorry, August."

August's ma took the news standing up. She twisted her apron and coughed out a sob but kept her head long enough to give orders.

"You'll have to git in there and bring your brother home. Lay him in the wagon and try to come on back without getting yer own self kilt. One in this day is all I can bear."

She turned to the house then where August knew she would commence her wailing. He saw Lucy standing in the doorway waiting, an expression of sober anticipation on her face, and he was glad she was here now. She had married Virgil a year ago last spring and had been a great help to Ma. Now this. Ma would need her more than ever.

August saddled his roan and headed over the hills toward Dry Branch. He had not mentioned a word to his mother that it just happened that today was his own birthday. He was nineteen. She probably forgot. Nineteen and a dead brother. He'd not forget that as long as he lived.

It took August an hour to get there, his mind working the whole time. He'd cried the first couple of miles, remembering all the things Junson had been to him. Brothers were brothers, but he and Junson had been closer than he and Virgil had been. Junson was twenty-three while Virgil was twenty-eight or twenty-nine. Lucy was only twenty. Virgil had hauled her out here from Bradley, the daughter of a teamster there. Pretty as a pine nut, Pa had said, when he first saw her. And she was.

In town he saw the wagon parked where Junson must have left it, directly in front of Amos's store. He edged his roan toward it and climbed down, tying the reins to the back of the wagon. Amos saw him and came out.

"Junson's in here," he said.

August climbed the wooden steps with a noticeable heaviness. Inside he saw the body lying across the door with the sheet pulled over him. "I come to git him home," he said.

"I figured."

"Pa and Virgil are in Bradley. Won't be home till tomorrow. Ma wants Junson back before they show up. It'll be better that way."

Amos nodded. "Grab that end, and I'll help tote him to the wagon."

It was a strange weight to August, a strange feeling to be packing both the burden of heaviness and the burden of grief. They slid Junson into the wagon then gently set him onto his side while Amos hefted the door out from under him.

August stood in awkward silence. "I'll need his rifle too."

"Oh. Sure. I'll get it."

While Amos was inside August walked out into the street and stopped where the dirt had been soaked black with his brother's blood. Mr. Leyland had appeared behind him now and August spoke to him without turning. "Where was the cowboy standin?"

Leyland pointed up the street to an overhang in front of the saloon. "He never went inside though. He just rode in. Seemed like he had killing on his mind from the start."

"He might have," August said. "They fought once. With fists."

Leyland showed surprise. "When did this happen?"

"Couple of weeks ago. It was at the water tank on the road to Garfield. Me and Junson come on Quinn taking a bath. He was striped to his waist, splashin water and soap all over himself."

Leyland stood there, waiting for August to continue.

"Junson asked what the occasion was. Was he getting

hitched or what? It was a joke. But it backfired, cause Quinn just smiled and said, 'Hell yeah. I'm getting hitched. To your gal Freya'. The laughin stopped then and they squared off. Junson knocked him around pretty good. Left him bloody. You know how Junson is. He is...*was*...good with his fists."

Leyland looked away. "There wasn't any laughing today. That cowboy was not looking for another beating." He took off his hat and wiped the sweat from inside the band. "Your pa isn't here?"

August shook his head.

"This will not be good," Leyland said. Both men turned when Amos returned with Junson's rifle.

"Lawman showed up," Amos said. "Came in right after it happened. But he hasn't done much. Asked a few questions is all. You might want to talk to him."

August shook his head. "Pa ain't going to listen to no lawman. Starkweather either."

Amos and Leyland glanced at each other. "Reckon not," Leyland said.

They watched in silence then as August climbed up onto the seat of the wagon. He nodded politely then snapped the leather and the wagon lurched up the dusty street, slowly rolling out of town.

In the wagon, all the way home, August fretted. He wished he could just keep going. He wished he could stop the wagon in front of the house, get back on his roan and just start riding. He truly did not want to be here when his pa got back. Junson was Pa's favorite. They all knew it. And now he was dead.

Douglas Starkweather stood on the wide veranda of the big house watching the thread of dust rising above the hill to the south.

A tall, dark man with a sharp, bladed face leaned against a corral gate. He had a distinctive star-shaped scar on his right cheek, just below the eye, and his neck was adorned with a yellow *a la Texas*-style silk scarf. He sang out, "The kid's comin in."

"I see him, Jack," Starkweather called back.

Both men stood waiting, neither saying another word, yet neither moving. They watched the rider finally break the crest of the hummock and race into the yard, only reining in his lathered horse until he was nearly upon the porch. Clouds of dust followed him in and swirled around as he leapt from the saddle. He took off his sombrero and slapped it against his leg, then gave out a whoop.

"It's done, boss."

Starkweather looked down at Brady Quinn and nodded gravely. His black, full-faced beard gave him an air of baleful authority. "Come inside. Have a drink. You too, Jack," he hollered to the dark man.

They followed him across the veranda, spurs jangling, and in through the wide heavy door. It was the first time Quinn had ever been inside his boss's imposing house and was immediately taken by its fulsome interior—the dark oak walls, the broad curtained windows, horsehair chairs, and a generous grouping of portraits and photographs on one wall. On another wall hung a map of the county, and draped from above the mantle was the tattered remains of a battle worn Confederate flag.

There was a tingling of glassware and bottles as Starkweather opened a cabinet and produced a tray of liquor. Looking up he saw young Quinn admiring the flag. Jack Stone, his black vest open in the front, a silver watch chain dangling from a breast pocket, remained standing by the door, silently watching Quinn. He was not a stranger to this room, nor was he a stranger to where the events of this day were headed.

Starkweather put the tray on a table and uncorked a decanter of amber whisky. He smiled. "That flag is all that remains of the Ridge Runners."

"The Ridge Runners?" Quinn tipped his hat back on his head quizzically.

Jack Stone stepped forward now, his fingers busy with a leather thong that hung from is gun belt. "Mr. Starkweather rode with General Jo Shelby."

Starkweather poured three glasses full of whisky and held one up. "Here's to General Jo," he said.

The other two men joined him, picked up glasses and raised them. When they were drained Brady Quinn, wide-eyed, said, "Ain't Shelby the feller that refused to surrender."

"The very same," Starkweather said. "He gathered a bunch of us up and took us deep into Mexico."

"Mr. Starkweather was captain in Shelby's Ridge

Runners."

Quinn stood dumbstruck. "I heard they killed more Apaches than—"

"Than anybody," Jack Stone said, cutting him off. "Killed the Apach. Killed greasers. Killed leftover Yanks. Ridge Runners would have killed their own mothers if they'd tried to strike a deal with the Union."

Starkweather poured another round of drinks. "Careful now, Jack. You'll scare the kid half to death with them old tales. Makes us sound uncivilized."

Jack Stone's dark smile was frightening enough. Brady glanced at the man, saw the ugly scar, and then turned quickly away.

"You handled Junson Tundel okay, did you?" Starkweather asked.

"He never saw it comin. I never give him a chance."

"He had a gun though?"

"Sure he did. That rifle he always carries. He was packin it."

"Any witnesses?"

"A few, maybe. I never really paid no mind."

Starkweather sipped his whisky and remained silent for a moment, his chin dipping into a faint nod. "There will be trouble though. Soon enough."

Stepping heavily to a desk in the corner of the great room, he pulled at a drawer and from its dim interior he retrieved two gold coins. Holding them in his outstretched hand he beckoned to Brady Quinn. "Here's the fifty I promised you. And...and another fifty for your loyalty, son."

The kid took both coins, stunned by the reality of them both being passed into his hands. "That's a lot of money, Mr. Starkweather."

Starkweather turned away from the kid's astonished embarrassment and went to the map on the wall. "You know where Benson's got a portion of the summer herd? Up above Frenchman Pass?" He pointed on the map to a raised grid.

Quinn nodded. "I was up there this spring. I helped drive them up. Remember?"

"Sure," Starkweather said absently. "I want you to hightail it back up there. Take a fresh horse. I need you to be out of sight for a while. Understand?"

Quinn nodded.

"Leave right away."

Quinn threw back the last of his whisky and headed for the door, then stopped. "Oh. There was a feller in town just about the time I busted Junson Tundel. He might of seen something."

"What kind of fellow?"

"He was old. Looked like he'd been on the trail a spell. Haggard. Started askin questions."

"What kind of questions?"

"Asked who I was ridin for. When I told him he asked if you was hirin?"

"What'd you tell him?"

"I told him, hell no you wasn't hirin."

"Anything else?"

Quinn thought. "Not really. Except. Except I didn't like

him."

Jack Stone spoke, his sharp face menacing from the shadows. "Probably some old saddle bum. There's a lot of them drifting around these days."

The kid nodded. "Maybe. But he seemed a little bit too sure of himself for that."

"Well, that's why I want you out of here," Starkweather said. "I'll send a rider up for you if I need you again. The whole east herd will be coming off the mountain in a week or two anyway. If you don't hear from me sooner, you can help Benson with the drive down."

No more words were spoken between them. Brady Quinn opened the big door and stepped back into the gathering twilight. Starkweather turned back to his map and smiled.

Jack Stone moved in behind him, toying with the leather thong on his holster. "You just birthed yourself a killer, Douglas. That kid'll ride through hell for you now."

From atop cemetery hill Boone Crowe had watched the boy ride into the town and then watched him leave again driving the wagon with his roan horse trailing behind. The wagon was carrying the load of the boy's kin. He could see the blanketed form in the back. He was glad he had not been down there for that bitter reunion. He'd seen more than enough of those.

Crowe turned and walked again among the graves that

had been spaced in familiar proximity to each other, as if in their deaths they still relished the comfort of each other's company. It was a small cemetery for a small town upon a small hill, and like most graveyards it was so chosen to afford the deceased a better view of the world they had once occupied.

He had left Hunter at the stable and walked up the side of the hill where a trail had been worn into the grass and dust. Fourteen graves total. He had counted each of them twice to be sure, and studied the names carved or painted upon the stones and wooden crosses. Several, it appeared, were from the same family, sharing the same last name. Several had dates indicating their old age or their infancy. But some were young folks. There was a Dorthea Hornfisher, a young woman. And a Hilton Bracket, a man in his seventies. And a pair of smaller graves bearing the names Lettie and Gunnar. No last names, presumably children. And a Lucia Ashmun, roughly forty. Lila Grove. She was thirty. And she had been dead for nearly ten years. This country had been hard on young women.

From this vantage point Boone Crowe could see all the way to the mountains; could see the distant, blackening clouds that held winter in their bellies. The green of summer was far-gone and most of what rolled across this plain now was the yellow and brown of mid-October. Snow and storms and freezing wind would come, as it always came in Wyoming, overnight, sudden as a thief. Then everything would hunker under the strain of it. The prairie would turn white, covering all but the horned buttes and hidden ridges of tall, golden-haired grass. The antelope and the deer and elk would come down and feed with the cattle herds and wagons and horses would fight the drifts. And back in Buffalo—where he wished he was now—there would be the heavenly warmth of the iron-grated stove in the lobby of the Occidental Hotel, and the idea of somebody unnamable sharing a room, and a bed, with him, all winter and maybe forever.

Foolishness, he thought.

And now he had stumbled into this unfortunate killing. It was that damn duty of his that forced him to tell the storekeeper that he was the marshal. He might well have rather done what Leyland had suggested—*just keep riding, mister.* But now he was in the middle of something that would probably require the law, and that wasn't why he was here. He was looking for someone and Dry Branch, Wyoming Territory, wasn't the place he wanted to be slowed down.

Below he could see a coyote creeping through the tall brush behind Amos' mercantile and the shabby building next to it that passed itself off as a hotel. It was the trash heap back there that the coyote hoped to invade, but it skulked cautiously, watching closely for any man or dog that might sound the alarm. It must have a den nearby with pups. And just east of the trash heap, directly behind the livery stable, where young Tanner had housed Hunter, Crowe studied the strange shack that bordered the hog pens. It was a crude affair, not unlike many he had seen in other undersized towns in the territory. But this one had the unusual addition of ropes that lead first from the front door of the shack out across open ground to the hog pens, and another rope leading from the pig trough into the back door of the livery barn. A final rope was attached from the shack door out back to the outhouse.

Odd, he thought.

The coyote, in full battle alert now, stole in close and put its snout into the midst of tin cans and old wrappers until it shook out a slab of something, looking from the hilltop like a hunk of rotting deer's flank. Pulling it out from the rest of the heap, the coyote then proceeded to drag its bounty backwards until it had once again reached the shelter of the thick sagebrush. Curving down into a grove of wild elms the coyote completely disappeared, presumably back down its den hole.

Moving back to the cemetery, Crowe retrieved his Winchester, which he had leaned against a tombstone, and then headed back down the trail and into the town and the trouble that waited there.

Not a word was spoken in the Tundel house. The only sound was that of water being sponged from a basin and onto the dead face and body of Junson Tundel. And later there was the dreadful screeching sound of the lantern hinge as it was lifted and the unusually loud flare of the match as it was struck into flame. The light then, coming from the lantern, threw a hideous melancholy against the walls and left grave and tragic shadows across the unmerciful expressions of Ma and Lucy as they stripped off the bloody clothes and redressed Junson into the respectable pants and shirt of his long ago confirmation garments. They had been let out by Lucy just last year so Junson could attend the dance in the Ashmun's barn this October last. That was where he had first spoken to Freya Ashmun.

August Tundel, sitting quiet and depressed in the dark corner watching this ceremony, suddenly realized that Junson would never again speak to Freya. Perhaps only he, August, knew of his brother's plans to ask Ward Ashmun for permission to court his daughter. All for nothing now. A dream turned to dust.

Chapter 2

BOONE CROWE LEFT Dry Branch early, riding east toward the creek, and then beyond to the Starkweather spread. In his saddle scabbard was the Winchester and on his hip was the old Navy Colt he had carried in the war and later had a gunsmith convert from a percussion pistol into a shell-chambered revolver. The black walnut grip was as familiar in his hand as the once-imagined touch of a certain fair woman. Inside, he hated such ridiculous comparisons, but in these, his old-man-desires, the thought of settling down alone, without the softer companionship of a—of *her*—held no lasting appeal at all. He wasn't getting soft; he was getting tired.

He found the creek and followed it north for a while then turned back east. All across the land was grass. Occasionally he would come to a grove of aspens, their leaves turning yellow against their white trunks, and further on he passed crowns of red rim rocks reflecting rusty red silhouettes against the morning sky. Even now, in these tailing decades of the century, Boone Crowe also kept an eye open for Indians. Most had been reduced to broken beggars by now, but a few proud bucks still banded together to steal cows from the ranchers, or fill a man caught alone with a passel of arrows just for the sport of it. In this hard country, beautiful as it was, ruthless men rambled. He had faced more than a few.

Before leaving the creek, Crowe let Hunter drink his fill.

Against the wind, which seemed always to be blowing, he picked up a scent of wood smoke and suspected that, because of its rich aroma, it was coming from a house. And true enough, within three-quarters of an hour he reined in atop a bluff that overlooked a great sprawling cattle ranch dotted with a network of corrals, as well as a colossal, three-story house. Bunkhouses and outhouses were scattered about the yard and from here he could see riders coming up to meet him. He sat his horse and waited.

"State your business," the first rider said as he pulled his horse up beside Crowe. Behind this man rode two others, each with a pistol at his hip, and one hand on the grip.

"You must be the welcome committee."

"I said, state your business."

Crowe studied this man, his floppy hat and grizzled beard, and a vague recognition swept over him. "Since when does a man need business to ride the range," he said.

"When you're on Starkweather range, it matters."

Crowe touched his chin in mock contemplation. "Starkweather. He the big man out here?"

The grizzled man looked hard at him.

"I don't remember seeing a sign that said to keep away."

"I'm telling you then. Unless you got business, keep away."

The other two riders edged their horses around so that Crowe was in the middle of their tightening circle.

The marshal shifted his reins from his right hand—his gun hand—over to his left hand, a movement noted by all three riders. He looked at the grizzled man and said, "You look like somebody I used to hate."

The man stiffened. "What the hell you mean?"

"Didn't I look down the sights of my rifle at you once? At Cold Harbor? I doubt I'd forget a face as ugly as yours."

In a rage the man fumbled for his pistol but almost magically, from under his coat, Boone Crowe whipped out another long barreled Colt and thrust it hard across the man's face, knocking him out of the saddle. Then pulling back on Hunter's reins, he turned instantly and pulled the hammer back on the pistol and aimed it pointblank in the face of one of the other riders. The third man held back. Crowe now had all three of them in front of him, the grizzled man sitting on the ground, dazed and spitting blood.

Slowly, Crowe shifted the hidden pistol to his left hand and drew the walnut handled pistol out of its sheath and held it in his right hand. "Now I've got my guns out and yours are still holstered. A much better arrangement, don't you think?"

"What're you after?" one of the other riders asked.

Crowe looked down at the grizzled man. "Looks like most of the fights gone out of him."

"You here to see Mr. Starkweather?"

"Maybe. If he's the boss."

"He's the boss."

"Well, I'm not too impressed, sending someone as stupid as your friend here to welcome visitors." He pointed a pistol at the grizzled man. "Do you know how close you just came to attending your own funeral?"

"Stow it, mister," said the second man, getting impatient

with all the talk.

Crowe looked at him. "It's not too late."

A long moment followed and Crowe felt that sick feeling in his gut, a feeling he knew too well, right before someone was about to do something foolish. They stared at each other, eyes unblinking, telltale.

"If your friend draws you'll all die. Do you know that?"

The moment dragged on. The third rider turned to his companion and said, "Don't."

Then the grizzled man, shaking his head, started to stand up. "Kill him," he grunted. The second rider drew then and Crowe shot him through the forehead, throwing him backward off his horse and onto the ground, his hat spinning off his head like a saucer and settling beside him. The third rider's horse reared, but he managed to stay in the saddle. He threw his hands out and shouted, "Don't shoot." The grizzled man, startled by the shot, fell back, digging his boot heels into the ground. The air stilled again, only eyes moving.

Crowe could see then that two more riders were coming up the hill from the ranch on the run. They waited for them to arrive in the eerie silence that always followed sudden, pointless death.

It was Starkweather himself, and Jack Stone, who reached the crest of the hill. Crowe kept his Colts out and leveled. Starkweather looked down at the grizzled man, then at the dead rider. "What happened here, Ike?"

Ike nodded his bloodied head nervously in Crowe's direction.

Starkweather turned then to the other rider. "Blake?"

Blake's eyes were cool and they fell onto his killed comrade. "This feller came up. Clint pressed him. First Ike, then Clint."

For the first time Starkweather looked at Crowe. "You killed one of my riders."

"It was very nearly all three."

Jack Stone laughed.

Blake shot Stone a hated look.

Starkweather touched the collar of his long gray broadcloth coat. He seemed to have lost interest in the dead man. His eyes turned to his visitor. "What brings you this far down, Crowe?"

The grizzled Ike bristled. "You know him, boss?"

Starkweather smiled unpleasantly. "Boone Crowe and I are old enemies."

Blake and Ike exchanged looks.

"You still lawing?" Starkweather asked.

Crowe could feel Jack Stone's eyes on him but he did not return the stare. "I am," he said. "But this time I'm on personal business."

"What kind of personal business has you riding across Double-Diamond range?"

"My business is at Fort Tillman. Last time I checked, it was due east."

Starkweather nodded. He saw Crowe's pistols still at the ready. "It seems a rather unfortunate thing that you picked this day to ride through."

"How's that?"

"Seems Clint here was just about to head north to help bring down the summer herd. Appears you left me shorthanded."

"I'd fill in for him if I wasn't on business. It's the least I could do."

Starkweather laughed. "You still have it, don't you, Crowe." He laughed again. "You're a hard man to hate. It'll be an unhappy day when you're finally gone."

Ike growled. "We could see to that right now."

Starkweather turned on him. "Shut up! And get this fool dragged out of here and put in the ground." Crowe wanted to give the grizzled man a lecture of his own, that death is a final act, and a loose and stupid tongue is the quickest way to it. But he said nothing.

With a nod then Starkweather pointed eastward. "The road to Fort Tillman is open to you, Marshal Boone Crowe. Happy traveling."

Crowe slowly holstered his Colts and nudged Hunter forward then stopped. "Oh, that reminds me. There was a killing in Dry Branch yesterday. Folks who saw it said it was one of your punchers did it. You know anything about that?" For the first time his eyes went to Jack Stone, to the yellow scarf at his neck, to the black suit coat and to the vile scar that rose like purple velvet across his cheek.

"Boys will be boys," Starkweather said.

Crowe nodded grimly. "I'll be in the area if you need me." Then, with a flick of the reins, he rode down the hillside through the lush yellow grass and followed the still red morning sun east.

The sedative given Freya Ashmun by Amos Bright was wearing off. Rising through that dark tunnel of troubled sleep she felt the warmth of the green-shaded light as it filtered across her face. Her eyes fluttered then closed again in dread when the black shadow of yesterday's memory fought past the medicine. Her sockets still burned from the many tears and her throat, dry from both drug and sleep, was sharp as a workman's rasp.

"Miss Ashmun?"

She started. Opening her eyes fully now she saw where she was—in one of Clive Leyland's hotel rooms—and sitting on a wooden chair in the dim corner was Little George, his fingers intertwined as if in prayer.

"I saw your eyelids movin," he said. "How you feelin? Mr. Leyland and Amos asked me to watch over you. Make sure you didn't wake up crying again."

"What…what time is it?"

"Closing in on noon. I've only been with you since nine. Mrs. Bright was with you. And Mrs. Evans the whole other time."

Slowly, with painful movement, Freya turned her legs over the side of the bed and sat up. "I need to wash my face, LG. Is there a basin in here?"

"Right here, missy. I'll fetch it."

"No. Not yet. I need to just sit a minute." She dabbed dumbly at her mussed hair then pulled at the ends of her fingers. "Is it true, LG? Or did I dream it?"

Little George dropped his head. "I wish we both had dreamed it. But it's so, I'm afraid, and we can't change it."

Freya held in her breath for a long time then let it out in a sad stream of reluctant acceptance. "Where is he now?"

"August come in and fetched him yesterday. He's home now. Waitin I reckon for the whole family to gather. His pa and Virgil was in Bradley."

She stood finally and walked unsteadily to the bureau where the basin set. Bending down she filled her cupped hands with water and brought it to her face. She did this many times before reaching for the towel that Little George held out to her. At last she walked to the window and peered through the green shade to the street below and the bitter irony of the dust, which blew from one end of the little town to the other.

"I need to find my father," she said finally.

"I'll have Matthew Hornfisher hitch up a buggy for you." He stood to go but she stopped him.

"He won't be at the house. He'll be on the west range. Numbering stock."

"I can ride up there. He won't be hard to find."

She shook her head. "That's kind of you, LG But I don't know what to do. I'm still not thinking straight. I'm...confused. I'm just so—"

At that moment there was a light knock, immediately followed by Mrs. Bright's face peering through the opening in the door. "Oh, good. You're awake. And feeling better, I hope."

Two miles east of Starkweather's ranch house, Boone Crowe pulled Hunter up and patted the horse's neck affectionately. Every few minutes he had checked the terrain behind him to see if he was being followed, but had seen no one. Neither had he looked upon the face of the dead Clint after he had hit the ground. He had to stay away from those kinds of intimacies. There were ghosts aplenty already crowding his dreams. He didn't need another.

Stepping from the saddle Crowe let Hunter graze for a spell while he tried to untangle his mind. Starkweather looked the same, well groomed, tightly shaven, only slightly silver at the temples. The long gray coat he wore was the give-away—still and always a Confederate, that old Ridge Runner brutality. One-on-one Crowe felt he could handle him, but Starkweather never did anything one-on-one. He always had his army around him. But that other character, that dark man with the Texas scarf. Crowe had not seen him before. Sure, he'd seen the type—cold, careful, cock-sure. A gunman in no hurry to prove it. This type liked the game of intimidation. Cat and mouse. Starkweather sees something he wants and takes it. This other fellow, I think he likes to play the game of the mind.

Crowe was reasoning most of this out loud to the horse, who knew his voice and seemed always to have an ear cocked to listen. Starkweather's army, he thought again. He hoped this Tundel family didn't try and go up against it.

"Hell," he spat.

The lawman cursed his luck for being caught in the middle of this mess now with so many other things on his mind. He wanted to get on to Fort Tillman. That's where his business was, or where he hoped he could at least get some answers. His only clue was a telegram, dated just months ago from Omaha. *Tomorrow I leave for Fort Tillman. Will visit a friend before coming on to Buffalo.* Tomorrow, he thought. What does tomorrow mean in a wild country like this. That Tundel boy used up his tomorrows. And so did that careless rider an hour ago. So many people rushing to die. Why am I still packing this badge? Haven't I had enough killing? Or am I just like the rest of them?

Crowe took up Hunter's reins again and climbed wearily into the saddle. He took another hard look over his shoulder, and then wheeled down into the ravine. Fort Tillman would have to wait another day. His duty now, as marshal, was to visit the Tundel farm and see if he couldn't ward off another killing.

"That damn Yankee dog," Starkweather said, reflecting bitterly. "We were both at Chickamauga. On odd ends of the barrage."

He and Jack Stone were leaning against a corral watching a rider handling a wild horse, and beyond, to a barren, treeless field where Ike and Blake labored at digging a grave.

"Crowe was a major in General Thomas' army. Get

Thomas planted and he was as rooted as a hickory." He gave a disapproving laugh. "I was detached to Hood at the time. They drove us clean off the field that day. Later, many of us fighting in the Wilderness got sent back east to help Lee. At Cold Harbor an artillery blast knocked me off my horse and it was Crowe put his saber under my chin. Took me prisoner. Once I got bunched with the other captives I slipped away. No discredit to Crowe. He could have run me through."

Jack Stone listened mutely.

Starkweather hooked his boot on the lowest rail of the corral. "Years later, riding with General Shelby, down to Mexico, Crowe was part of the federal detachment sent down to root us out. We came face to face a couple of times, Crowe and me. Out there in the desert. Even shot at each other a few times." He turned and looked directly at Jack Stone. "Don't be fooled. He's a tough old snake. Went into lawing some years back. I don't like that he's down here."

Jack Stone listened to Starkweather's tale with interest.

"Killing Clint was no stroke of luck," Starkweather went on. "And he wasn't lying when he said he could have killed all three of those boys. Crowe was a good soldier. He thinks things through."

"You want him out of the way?" Jack Stone said.

The two men looked at each other.

"It would make what I'm trying to do a whole lot easier. But he's nothing to mess with."

Jack Stone laughed. He drew out a pouch of tobacco from his shirt pocket and began rolling a cigarette, his hands cupped against the wind. "He's only one man."

Starkweather thought for a moment, and then said, "Let's see how things play out. No point jamming a stick in the hornet nest. Not if Crowe clears out in a day or two on his own."

"And if he doesn't?"

"Then we proceed as planned. If enough Tundels die, then we don't need to waste our time burning them out. By then, what's left of them will leave without further encouragement."

Jack Stone smiled. "Oh, but I do like those big fires. Especially at night when they light up the whole sky. Red sparks rising in the black sky. Why, done right, it can be a thing of beauty." He drew in deeply on the cigarette. "And speaking of beauty. That young Tundel woman. She's a thing to look at."

Starkweather nodded approvingly. "They can make a man tremble, can't they?"

Jack Stone laughed, blowing smoke into the wind. "My weakness, I'm not ashamed to say. My only weakness."

"Killings not your weakness?"

"Killing is my business—my gift. Women? They're the happy dividend. Behind most killing stands a woman."

Starkweather seemed momentarily lost in thought but nodded absently. The tails of his long coat fluttered in the wind like a restless regimental flag. Silence followed, both men gazing off toward the field where the two riders were now lowering the canvas-wrapped body of Clint into their fresh hole.

Finally Jack Stone said, "And then there's Ashmun."

The name brought Starkweather back around. "Ashmun can wait. I have my own ideas about him. First the Tundels. Then Ward Ashmun."

"And what if your friend Marshal Crowe just happens to get caught in a crossfire?"

Starkweather smiled. "Well, then, all the better."

Brady Quinn tried to sleep in the saddle but it was no good. He hadn't gotten a wink the night before either. The shack at Frenchman Pass was inhospitable to sleep, cold, drafty and filled with smoke from a poorly ventilated chimney. In warmer weather he would have slept outside on the ground, but at this height the nights were getting cold, and the chance of a rattlesnake crawling into your bedding was increasing with the weather. And then Benson had wakened him at midnight to do the night watch, so here he was, sleepless and filled with thoughts.

He had ridden here straight away, just as Mr. Starkweather had ordered, arriving near dark. Benson and Yarlott were with the cattle and when Quinn came into the shack Dibbs was sitting on his bunk, still wearing his furry chaps, trying to read a book by candlelight.

"Well, I'll be. If it ain't the kid," squawked Dibbs cheerfully, looking up from the page. "You get demoted or something?"

Quinn threw his kit onto an empty bunk and kicked at a

tin can that littered the floor.

"I see you're in your usual humor," Dibbs said.

"Where's everybody?"

"Where'd you think? They're up above, starin at the backside of cows."

The kid walked to the only window and peered into the gathering darkness.

"Don't worry," Dibbs said. "You'll get your chance tonight. You and me. Night watch. Nice and quiet. Unlest it rains."

"It rained a bit comin up," Quinn said.

"That a fact." He pointed to the wall where two slickers were draped from pegs. "There hangs our salvation."

Now, hours later, true enough, he was wearing one of those slickers under the steady, dark drizzle of a gray morning, the cattle lowing calmly. Through the gray rain Quinn could barely make out Dibbs, sitting his horse, the broad silhouette of his sombrero and the red spark of his cigarette where the hidden shadow of his face was.

This won't do, he thought. Not for another month.

He reached under the slicker until his hand found the butt of his pistol and he caressed it fondly. Junson Tundel, dropping in the street like he did, had played over and over in his mind during the ride up here. *Make it look good*. That's all Mr. Starkweather had said. *Make it look good.* And so he had. For a while before, and for a while after, he thought it might rattle him. But what he felt wasn't fear or bad conscience. It was something else. He'd done a killing for Mr. Starkweather and Mr. Starkweather had paid him good for his work. So that's what it was. Work. It was a job—a killing job.

There was that look, from Blake, right before he'd headed into Dry Branch.

"Where you off to?" Blake had said.

"To settle a score," Quinn said.

"You goin to get your ass whipped again by Junson?"

Quinn had smiled back bravely. "I'll let you know."

Well, he hadn't told Blake. Hadn't told anybody. He'd just gathered his tack and rode. But word would get back to Blake, eventually.

"Here's your ass-whippin," he said to himself now. "This day there'll be cryin at the Tundel homestead."

"Who're you jabberin at, kid?"

It was Dibbs. He'd ridden up silently on his flank.

For a moment Brady Quinn felt a strange and sudden desire to lift his pistol from his holster and blow a hole clean through Dibbs. Not from anger. He surely liked Dibbs alright. He was always reading some book and repeating lines from it. And his Johnnycakes were the best he'd ever eaten. No. Quinn felt like killing him for a whole different reason, and his eyes grew menacing in realizing it. Less than twenty-four hours ago he'd killed his another man. This ominous shadow that hovered over him now was the realization that he wanted to kill again.

"Rain's lettin up. Wouldn't you know it. Benson and Yarlott'll probably have a dry watch."

Quinn felt his face turning hot and he wanted to throw off the slicker and face him. He wanted to see Dibbs scared.

He hadn't gotten to see Junson Tundel scared. There hadn't been any time for that. He'd just shouted his name and then drew and shot. And Junson would not have been scared anyway. But Dibbs would. He was peace loving as a turnip. All he knew was cows and books. He'd be scared alright.

"What you dreamin on? You doin arithmetic numbers in your head or somethin? Or is it a girl?" Dibbs chuckled. "That's it, ain't it? A girl."

At the mention of a girl Quinn suddenly saw Freya Ashmun's face. And then he heard her scream. After Junson had fallen Freya Ashmun had run into the street, wailing like a calf, and it all played back to him now. Her blonde hair half-undone. Her riding pants scuffed where she knelt in the street. Her high black boots. And her face, all twisted into sobbing. He remembered how for an instant he thought he should just shoot them all. Amos Bright. That Leyland fellow. Even that trembling little kid.

But her?

Her white skin came to him now, the way it showed beneath her neck, and he knew he could never kill her. It had excited him to see her crying. He would like to see that again. And to touch her. He'd like to put his hands where no man probably had. Not even Junson Tundel. She was a wild flower he'd like to smell. And then pluck.

Quinn's hand relaxed from his pistol grip. "Damn, Dibbs, if you didn't read my mind."

The old man, Ernest Tundel, and his son, Virgil, saw the unfamiliar horse tied up to the garden gate and they exchanged a look.

"Seen that critter before?" the old man asked.

"Never," said Virgil.

They had just come in from the north, the only safe passage from Bradley without running into Starkweather riders. There had been rain to the east but they had missed it and now, coming up on their homestead, a welcome sun threw its broad shadows across the yard. There was a rifle poking out of a saddle scabbard on this strange horse, and this bay had just then lifted its head at the sound of the two approaching Tundels. The sound of their cautious hoof beats brought a figure to the open doorway of the house. It was August. When they reached the yard and dismounted, August came up to them.

"I'll tend the horses. Ma needs you inside," he said, not looking at their faces.

"Whose horse is this?" Ernest Tundel asked.

"He's inside, Pa." Then August took the reins and led the horses to the barn. He looked once over his shoulder as his father and brother entered the house, then he saw the flash of calico where Lucy passed to Virgil, touching his shirtsleeve. Then August turned away and began loosening the cinches on both horses and pulled off their saddles. He could hear the muffled sound of voices but could make out no distinct words, until his father's deep and clear voice carried out—"No!"

It was later. The sun had hit its crest and was now slanting westward. The whole family was sitting around a table that had been placed in the front yard. No one was eating but there was coffee and the men fidgeted with their mugs, occasionally lifting one to drink. Marshal Crowe sat at one end of the table watching the protracted sadness on the gathered faces. He wanted to be on his way, but felt obligated to sit through some of this misery with them.

"Don't bother getting the judge," the old man said. This was directed at Crowe even though his eyes never left the tabletop.

"Marshal, we know what they're after," Virgil said, pointing toward the creek. "And it isn't that water. Starkweather can get to that water easy enough, with or without us. And this land is of no particular value either, except…" He paused and then swept his arm westward. "Except it stands between him and the real prize. Ashmun's spread. Its Ashmun's range he wants. He wants it all."

There was deep bitterness in these words and Virgil's face showed a redness that punctuated that bitterness. "We've had no law here since that deputy Lacrosse lit out near a year ago. Just as well. Starkweather got to him and scared him off."

Crowe was aware of the deputy's disappearance but decided to let the subject drop. Instead he studied the old man, trying to detect any sign of brash behavior; any indication he might take the law into his own hands. The old man's noble gray mustache hung from his long face, his blue eyes fully darkening—more from grief at this moment than from rage—and his big head and rumpled hair showed a mix of thoughtfulness and defeat.

Finally Boone Crowe spoke. "Your boy August here says you've lost neighbors."

Virgil laughed sardonically. "If they don't leave on their own, they get burned out. Follow this creek north a few miles, Marshal, then northeast. You'll find the burnt ruins of two farms." He glared at Crowe. "And we're next. Killing my brother was just their opening move. They'll be waiting to see what we do."

Once again, the table fell silent. For a short time the day had turned warm, as if in a false effort to ease the suffering of this family. Crowe could smell the odor of livestock behind him but it did not displease him. It was his wish still that he might someday finally leave this badge and settle to some final years of peaceful agriculture. In fact, when his private business in this part of the territory was complete, it may very well hasten the fulfillment of that wish.

The elder Mrs. Tundel went into the house and a clatter of pans was heard from the kitchen. August used this moment to look at his brother's wife, Lucy, and it appeared to Crowe, who observed this, that the young Tundel was feeling pity for her. Pity, or perhaps a presentiment of added sorrow for having found herself a living member of this troubled family. When Ma Tundel returned she feinted at being hospitable, pouring more coffee from a big flame-blackened pot, but her lips were tight and silent.

Crowe shifted in his chair. "Mr. Tundel. May I ask you a personal question?"

Tundel lifted his great head and looked at the marshal.

"Did you serve in the war?" Crowe asked.

The old man's eyes appeared suddenly to set on a point in eternity. He stroked his mustache absently. "I did."

Crowe hesitated, and then asked, "On the winning side?"

"I did," he said again.

"Do you ever think about the war?"

"I try very hard not to."

Crowe nodded understandingly. "But Starkweather, he did not fight for the winning side. He fought—and very determinedly—for the losing side. Unlike you and me, Starkweather tries very hard *never* to forget. It has remained a sort of second life for him."

"Why you telling us this," Virgil asked bitterly.

"I just want you to know what kind of man you're up against. Starkweather's good side, if he ever had one, was left buried on a battlefield somewhere. To him, and most of the men he surrounds himself with, the war never ended. Alone, you'll likely not win."

"What do you suggest? That we sit here and do nothing. Almost every day there's a Starkweather rider sitting on one of those ridges, watching us," Virgil said.

"Let em watch. As long as he isn't shooting at you, just go about your business. The first sign of trouble by you, they'll swarm down here and it'll be over in an hour."

"That's poor advice if you ask me."

"I don't have any other to give you. For the time being, you need to fortify this place. Work up a plan to defend yourself from inside these walls. I'll be riding to Fort Tillman as soon as I leave here. I have business there. I'll try and find some good stock that I can deputize. If we get enough men here, we might be able to buy some time."

"Time," Virgil spat. "My brother is layin on the table in there from a Starkweather bullet and you're telling me to sit tight. You can go to hell, Marshal."

With these words Virgil stood up, but the voice of Ernest Tundel broke through. "Sit down, son. Going crazy now isn't goin to bring Junson back."

A look passed between father and son then, a look that disturbed Boone Crowe, but enough had been said, so he let it pass. He was only one man. And it was time for him to leave.

August Tundel stood silently and walked to Hunter, stroking the horse's mane. When the marshal came to him he untied the reins and handed them to the lawman. The others at the table rose also and one-by-one they walked through the door and into the house. All except Lucy, who stood but only stared, as in a trance, at the cluttered table and the half-empty cups. Both men looked at her then at each other.

"She's feeling what I'm feeling," August said in a low voice. "That there's more bad coming."

Ike Werth's wrecked face was swollen and still bleeding in places, the imprint of Crowe's Colt still visible across the bridge of his nose. Starkweather had shown no sympathy for him and after he and Blake finished with Clint's grave, he had been instructed to ride the line looking for mavericks.

"You're lucky you're still breathing," Starkweather told him.

Ike cinched up his saddle and rode over the northern slope, his mind on killing the old lawman that'd made a fool of him. At the same time Starkweather ordered Blake to ride over toward the Tundel place and keep an eye on things.

"I want to know if those punkin-rollers are arming for a fight. Or if they're packing up their belongings." He said this with a satisfied smile.

Blake said nothing, only pulled his hat down over his brow, wheeled his horse and rode off. Unlike Ike, Blake's mind was not on killing anybody. He had signed on to cowboy, not get in the middle of a shooting war. And with Clint dead he saw how close it was.

Behind Amos Bright's store, the declining sun, tipping behind the Sawtooth range, was already throwing a brilliancy of pink and gold traces across the sage hills. The air was holding its last warmth and Freya Ashmun, blonde hair tied back and broad-brimmed riding hat balanced on her knee, sat alone on Amos's back porch. She had tried several times to have her horse saddled and to ride home, but each time she lacked the will needed to do anything but remain inactive and mournful. Junson Tundel had not been her lover. Not yet. They had only just begun exchanging teasing glances and remarks. She found him handsome and daring. A little like the heroes in the Walter Scott books she read, a room full of them, first read and then left behind by her mother before she died. She, herself, was trying to live in just such a brave fashion, like the heroines who had disguised themselves as men in these stories, and fought with both sword and pistol for one kingdom or another. But the killing of Junson yesterday reduced all such fantasies to dust. There had been no heroics in his dying. He had not even lifted his rifle in defense. There had been no time. He only raised his head in response to his called name.

Movement from the kitchen door of the Hornfisher house woke her from her reverie. It was Tanner, emerging from the doorway, carrying a tin plate of food. She watched him cradle it carefully in his small hands, as he did every evening, fetching it past the hog pens and the stretched ropes to the front door of the little shack out back. She watched him walk with care, balancing the plate as if it contained eggs, or gold, or something even more precious. Once at the shack he gingerly tapped the bottom of the door with his boot until it opened a crack and two brown hands reached from the shadows and received it. Then followed the high-pitched screech of unintelligible words, as if croaked out by a throttled parrot.

Tanner was halfway back to his house before he looked up and saw Freya and she instantly waved him over. He obeyed her beckoning, shyly, and stood before her now with gloomy face.

"We must be brave, Tanner Hornfisher," she said. She said this with weak conviction.

Tanner said nothing in reply, his eyes darting uneasily.

"We both lost…a good friend." Her voice quivered, and she wished now that she'd never spoken, new tears burning her eyes.

The boy's face crumpled then and Freya instantly rose, dropping her hat, and she came to him, wrapping him in her arms. She put her hand on the back of his dusty hair and pulled him close to her neck and together they cried, as if the whole bleak world had come to roost on their tormented shoulders.

He realized he would not make Fort Tillman on that day, he'd spent too many hours with the Tundel's, so Boone Crowe gazed the landscape for a place to make a small camp. It was just as well. He was already nearly done-in by the long four-day ride from Buffalo and these latest events had only added to his weariness. Ahead, about a quarter of a mile, on the west side of a knoll, was a cluster of aspens, and he stirred Hunter in that direction. Sleeping on the ground was not the same as sleeping in a bed but as tired as he was it probably wouldn't make a difference.

The aspen leaves were in color and rustling in the breeze as he pulled the saddle from Hunter and turned him out to graze. This horse was as close to being a human than any he'd ever known and he was never worried about the animal straying off. More human than many humans, he thought. He hadn't known any horse that deliberately set out to murder another, the way men did. And it was beginning to look as though that is exactly what this Quinn cowboy did when he came gunning for Junson Tundel. Was it jealousy? August Tundel had said something about a girl and Boone had assumed it was the young gal that he'd seen crying in the street.

Or was it pure meanness? Some of these cowboys were orphans with their lives written on the water. Living into old age was not a thing to be grasped. Or maybe even desired. Some of them had come up from Texas to work on these big spreads and were packing with them a dark hatred against the whole wide world. Many of them were the stray children of the Civil War dead. And it sure didn't help a kid like Quinn to fall in with the likes of Starkweather, whose own wartime bitterness still roared like a furnace inside him.

The farmers, few as they might actually be, and stretching across many miles, had come to Wyoming with no hidden agenda except to raise their hay, some food crops, and run stock. Not big herds, twenty maybe, or fifty, only enough to supply themselves with meat, or to trade or sell a few. They held no grudges and generally got along.

Boone Crowe knew all of this. His job, out of the rough, saloon-infested town called Buffalo, was keeping the peace, or chasing down an occasional robber or horse thief. These were typically stupid men and easy to track. Killings were usually ignited by old grudges or the unthinking result of whisky, and sometimes, but not always, over a woman—hardly ever a good woman.

But these last years had seen an increase in the big cattle operations, many foreign owned and run by arrogant land grabbers who had connections with bankers and politicians. These big outfits were taking over the range and inciting fights with the farmers, oftentimes over barbwire fences or sheep or water. And there was this trouble with mavericks, the unbranded calves and yearlings, and the constantly raised question of ownership—if a maverick was straying the range, who could claim it? And was claiming it, with an unregistered brand, the same thing as rustling? Rustling, in itself a desperate occupation, was on the increase, giving vengeful ranchers and their cowboy hirelings, an excuse to form vigilance committees—a sophisticated name for a lynch mob—to track and hang anyone they thought might be a rustler. These incidents were rarely reported to either lawmen or judges. Only last April, Crowe had stumbled onto a lynching party and when he tried to intervene the mob's guns were turned mockingly in his direction, fearing neither him nor his badge.

Now, here was Starkweather, perhaps the most ruthless of men, trying to build his own empire in Wyoming territory.

Boone Crowe reflected on these things as he built a small fire from broken sage branches and applied himself to the making of coffee. He felt he had given Tundel poor advice. Turning a farm into a fortress seemed desperate but until he knew more about the shooting of Junson Tundel, and the reasoning behind it, waiting it out seemed all the family could do. He wasn't sure, if the tables were turned, that he could even follow his own advice. It all hinged on the old man. Would he give himself time to grieve, while watching the horizon for trouble? Or would he go off half-cocked and find himself as dead as his son?

He threw a stick on the fire. "I'm only one man," he said out loud.

Later, in his sleep, the face of the woman came to him and he stirred restlessly. He called out something unintelligible and Hunter, dozing under an aspen, suddenly lifted his head. The night was clear and cold and the last trailing of smoke from the fire lifted like a thin whisper against the sky. Two miles away, riding slowly in the moonlight, Ike Werth was rejoicing in his unexpected good fortune. He believed he had stumbled upon what appeared to be the marshal's fresh trail. Every few minutes he dismounted and examined the track, making sure he didn't lose it in the dark.

Virgil Tundel lay in the tall bluestem and stared at the rider silhouetted against the moon. He had been watching for nearly an hour, not moving, but neither had the rider moved, only sat his horse, hunch-shouldered, gazing down into the dark Tundel yard. Virgil held the Big Fifty—the Sharps that his father had used in the war—close to his side. Earlier he had turned over in bed and whispered to Lucy, who seemed to be sleeping fitfully, that he was going out to look around. *Don't go,* she'd said, but he ignored her and slipped into his clothes and coat and crept out of their detached room and strode across the yard to the barn.

Old man Tundel had said to wait, but Virgil could not. His brother was dead and he was determined to take the fight to them. To that Quinn fellow. To Starkweather. To anyone who tried to stop him. And that included that gray-whiskered old lawman. Hell, he thought that tin star was probably halfway back to Buffalo by now, breathing a sigh of relief to be out of here. The moon was high. It was time. He rested his left elbow on the ground and slid the Sharps up, securing the stock firmly against his shoulder. He pivoted, using his hand to spread the grass in front of him, and then tried, in the dark, to sight down the black barrel. There he was, the rider, sitting against the moon like a duck in a silver pond. Without gloves his finger was cold, but he slipped it into the trigger guard and squeezed.

Blake did not hear the report before the bullet creased his skull. Only by his cowboy instincts was he able to stay in the saddle as the panicked horse twisted and bucked. There was no pain yet, but an instant dizzying distress overwhelmed him and he could feel his head involuntarily loll, like the floppy head of a rag doll. He held feebly to the reins, already disoriented, wondering, without hope, where the shot had come from. At last he simply wheeled the horse completely around and began riding downhill, away from the homestead and into the darkness. He heard another husky report from the Sharps but saw no flash and knew it had missed. Feeling weak he hung over the saddle, trying to hold the horse's neck, while the horse, with its own reins, bolted across the dark range and into the deepening night.

Chapter 3

IT WAS NOT yet daylight. Ike Werth came out of the foggy morning mist on foot and moved amidst the bramble toward the grove of aspens. He had brought no rifle but he had his pistol and it was drawn now and aimed in the direction of the fading ashes of campfire and the blanketed form beside it. In the distance behind him he could hear his own horse nicker. Nothing stirred. At twenty paces he raised the pistol and the quiet morning exploded with the sound of three quick gunshots. Birds flew from the treetops and the echo of the reports soared and scattered as if they too had wings.

Lips curling, Ike strode to the bullet-riddled bedroll and kicked it with his boot, uncovering a twist of sage branches and tufts of grass. Then, from the trees came the clear metallic clack of a Winchester's lever action, and he froze.

There followed an eternity of silence and Ike fidgeted, trying hard to squint into the gray darkness. Finally Boone Crowe's voice floated out from the thickets, deep and even-toned.

"Use that iron. Or pitch it."

Ike threw the pistol into the dirt, tossing it away as if it were a live snake.

"You don't seem quite as eager to kill me now."

Ike sputtered something unintelligible.

Finally Crowe materialized out of the mist, his rifle pointing directly at Ike's middle. "You made a bad mistake following me here," he said. "Attempted murder of a federally appointed peace officer. That's a hanging offense."

Ike's open jaw clamped shut, his tongue flapping noisily as if he were trying to work up enough spit to speak. "Yer word 'gainst mine."

"Your trial wouldn't last three minutes. They'd string you up."

"What're you aimin to do?" His breathing becoming labored.

Crowe walked out of the shadows and the circled silver star pinned to his vest blinked in the twilight.

"I don't know yet. I haven't decided. If you hadn't made more noise than a one-legged duck I might be dead now. But I'm not. The proper thing would be to take you in to Fort Tillman and have you hanged."

"Starkweather…wou…wouldn't like that," he stammered.

"Starkweather doesn't give a rabbit's ass about you. You're stupid and you're a coward. And Starkweather knows it just like I know it. No. Killing you would be doing him a favor."

Ike's eyes flashed, and they darted around trying to find where he had thrown his pistol. He wished he had it in his hand now.

"I thought I was done with you. You went and got your friend killed yesterday. Now here you are, getting fresh all over again."

They stood glaring at each other for a long moment. Ike's still-swollen face from the day before was puffed and scabbed above the nose. Finally Crowe glanced down at his bedroll and at the three bullet holes in it and a rage worked its way up through his legs and into his arms. Without warning he stepped up and heaved the butt of his Winchester against the side of Ike's head, knocking him to the ground.

"Understand this," he said. "I could put a bullet in you right now. Then I could crawl back in that sack and sleep like a baby. The coyotes could drag off your bones and I'd still be dreaming of women and beer."

He kicked him then, hard in the ribs and Ike groaned. Then he placed the barrel of the rifle to the rider's temple and he held it there, the cold steel pressing against his skull.

Ike's resolve finally broke and he whimpered. "Don't...please..."

Crowe waited a long time before pulling the rifle back. The rage had turned his throat tight and his tongue felt thick, his own temples flushing red with fury. "I believe I will kill you. Someday. In fact, if I ever see you again I will kill you. Now stand up."

The beaten rider rose cautiously and clumsily to his feet.

"Now get out of them clothes."

"What?"

"You heard me. I want those clothes off."

He raised the rifle again and Ike flinched. Then he pulled off his coat, then his bandana.

"Everything."

The shirt came next, then the boots and pants, until he stood there in only his filthy red long underwear and his hat.

"Where's your horse?"

"Over...yonder."

"I'll be taking him with me."

"What? You...can't...it's a two day walk to..."

"I'll leave your boots a mile up the trail. It'll be your job to find them."

"That's horse-thievin."

"Would you rather ride your horse to Fort Tillman and get your neck stretched? Now turn around." He placed the Winchester against Ike's right ear until the rider turned around. The trap door of his long underwear was held shut by three buttons. Crowe reached down and ripped each button off from its thread and the trap door fell open, revealing the rider's furry rear end.

"I want your brains to be showing when you walk into Starkweather's ranch house. And I want you to tell him what I told you. That I'll kill you if I ever see you again. Now start walking. I got no more time for you."

"What about my boots? You said—"

"I know what I said." He kicked the boots, one by one, in Ike's direction. "I'm feeling generous," he said, and he watched as the rider pulled them on over his foul bare feet.

It took ten minutes for Ike to walk out of sight, and the sun was fully up by the time Boone Crowe had gathered up the two horses, Ike's pistol, the shot-through bedding, and was at last in the saddle again, heading for Fort Tillman, still a half day's ride away.

August Tundel spent the morning helping his pa build the box for Junson. They wanted him buried by sundown, so they labored in the barn with planes and saws, hammers and nails, neither of them speaking, their sorrowful eyes directed only at their work. Virgil had been out with them earlier, but only for a few minutes. There were tense words spoken between the old man and Virgil and at one point Virgil challenged his father openly.

"That will not do, Pa. We will all be next. Soon enough."

Ernest Tundel clutched the plane in his hand, blonde shavings of white pine falling from the blade. "Do you think I don't know that? I am not blind. And no, I do not expect to sit back. But we will sit back long enough to put your brother respectably into the ground. Going out and shooting at Starkweather's riders will only hasten our ruin. I fear this very minute but what your stupid act last night has caused."

"Pa! A stupid act?" He gestured toward August and said, "Just Sunday you had three sons. Now you have only two."

Ernest shook the plane in his son's face. "Do you think your pain is greater than mine? Greater than your mother's? It is not a thing that gets wiped out just because you start your own killing. Before this is over you will have all the killing you can stand. It will come to that and I know it. But today belongs to Junson. Now go water the corn. Or check the fences. Or cut the hay. Do something. But save your killing for another day."

Virgil stomped from the barn, pulling his hat off his head and beating his leg with it as he went.

Later, after the coffin was finished and the grave opened,

a queer stillness came upon the farm. All life, both man and animal, seemed suspended on the unsavory threshold of apprehension, a colossus of nameless disorder. A chill breeze swept down the hill and rattled the corn stalks and even the cattle turned, as if recognizing the omen, and stood in unified bewilderment. August, packing a bucket of water from the well to the house looked up and saw Lucy watching him, her grim, handsome face showing an unguarded expression of fretfulness. She watched him carry it into the house and she followed him there, seeming to study him as he placed the bucket onto the table, but she said nothing to him. He turned to face her and their eyes fluttered briefly, not quite engaging, then she looked away and went out.

Blake woke, his face buried deep into the rustling bluestem, his left arm twisted beneath him and his legs splayed like a wishbone. He tried to raise his head but let it drop back down. Conscious now, he laid still trying to collect his senses. After a time he pulled his pinned arm out from under him and lifted it to his head. Dried blood. There was even a furrow on the left side of his skull, neat as if someone had plowed it there. At last he rolled onto his back and blinked at the sun.

Nothing moved but the grass.

A cattleman, perched atop a hill in Wyoming, can see a long way off. And if that cattleman is Ward Ashmun, he believes, just as Douglas Starkweather believes, that any land where his cattle range, that land belongs to him. But that is a fallacy. Some big cattlemen did come early, and some did help wrestle the land from the Indian's grasp, but they, just like the Indian, had no legal claim to it. Possession. That was their claim.

When men like Ernest Tundel came along, they carried with them an actual deeded title to 180 acres, land of their own choosing, courtesy of the federal government. They tore up some of the grass and built houses and planted gardens. They fenced off pastures, grew patches of corn, some wheat and mostly hay. They had milk cows, a few sheep, some workhorses and some riding horses and maybe a mule, and some ran small herds of their own cattle. They came to raise a family and to prosper, and in so doing they became the instant enemy of the big stockmen.

On this late morning Ward Ashmun was standing by his chuck wagon drinking a tin cup of black coffee and waiting for his daughter's hysteria to pass. She was still sitting astride her borrowed horse, which had made the long ride from Dry Branch from daybreak. At that moment she was crying less from the death of Junson Tundel than from her father's reaction to it.

"Just as well," he'd said, in a matter of fact way. "Maybe they'll pull out now."

"How can you say that?"

Ashmun rarely engaged in emotional conversation with his daughter. He was a severe realist. Any chance of him maneuvering through the tricky terrain of sentimentality had left him the day his wife died, several years earlier. He was nothing now but a course, passionless ruler of the open range, and his daughter's flights of fancy were an unwelcome distraction.

"You might get off that animal and give it a rest," he said, tossing the last dredges of his coffee onto the ground. "Whose horse is it?"

Freya pushed through her frustration and wiped her tears with the heel of her palm. "One of Matt Hornfisher's." Her tone was angry.

Ashmun looked off across the slope to where his cowboys were meandering alongside several hundred grazing beeves. His foreman, Wes Bridges, was staring at him with a mocking, mustachioed grin. Bridges was well aware of the temperamental sixteen-year-old girl and knew also of the fits it sometimes offered his boss. *What the hell do I know about raising a girl,* he'd said, when Freya was only ten and they had just put her mother in the ground. Bridges, who was just another cowhand then, knew, from having grown up with sisters, that old man Ashmun had met his match. It tickled him now to know that six years had not changed anything.

"What the hell you staring at?" Ashmun yelled. His voice churned like gravel from decades of shouting over bawling cattle and fierce Wyoming gales.

Bridges laughed out loud, spurring his horse closer.

"Boss. You better put your brand on that maverick before somebody else does."

Freya tossed her head in indignation.

"Your business is cattle. Not women. See to it."

Wes Bridges withdrew. He pulled out a pouch of tobacco and feinted making a cigarette, but then put the whole kit away without lighting up. He pulled his horse around and rode across the flat, leaving a dry dust behind.

Ashmun strode to the chuck wagon and untied the reins of his horse. He took off his big hat and brushed his fingers through his charcoal hair. He pulled a handkerchief from his pocket and swiped at the sweat on the inside band of his hat, then pulled it back on his head. Ashmun stuck his worn boot into the stirrup and swung up into the saddle and there, like a monarch, surveyed this small percentage of his vast herd. In the ravine, he saw Wes Bridges was barking orders to the riders, and Ashmun knew he had made the foreman angry. It's a good thing, sometimes, to put them in their place, he thought. He nudged his mount over to where Freya's horse stood, and gave her a satisfied look.

Fury robbed her of words. She jumped from her tired horse and let the loose reins trail in the grass. At the chuck wagon she found a bag of potatoes and grabbing one she reared back and threw it hard at her father who had already turned and was riding away. The potato hit him on the back but he showed no reaction, only prodded his horse into a trot and disappeared over a grassy hummock, leaving her to fume in icy solitude.

A small army of riders, led by Starkweather himself, crossed over the creek and headed up the far slope in the direction of the Tundel farm. His man, Tee Blake, had not returned with his report during the night, nor had he come back this morning. If there had been trouble, Starkweather was ready for it. But halfway there they spied a lone rider on the horizon and they pulled up their mounts and waited.

"That's Blake's hoss, alright," one of the riders said.

"Sure enough. That's old Tee," joined another.

Starkweather nodded.

They watched him approach and as he drew near they saw that he was hatless and that he had a piece of cloth tied around his head.

"What happened?" Starkweather asked, riding out to meet him.

After a long morning of headache and wobbly legs, Blake had caught up with his horse, and then washed off his bloody head in a half-dried cow wallow. Then for another long hour he sat by the muddy water, trying to shape some mental picture of what his future might be. He was a cowboy, not a gun hand. Forty dollars a month for punching cows in bad weather was barely enough as it was. Being target practice for a sodbuster's buffalo gun had never been part of the mix. Not his mix anyway. There were jobs in Montana, he thought. But even as he saddled up and gingerly headed back to the ranch, he knew that Starkweather was no man to trifle with. Everything he owned was back in the Double-Diamond bunkhouse: his saddlebags, his plaid shirts and wooly chaps, fancy boots and Spanish spurs, his ropes, his other pony, and the small tobacco tin of cash—his meager, hardscrabble grubstake. But Tee Blake's mind was made up.

Now here was Starkweather, with his lackey, Jack Stone, and a dozen riders, their chests puffed out and ready for a fight.

"Had a fall," Blake said.

"A fall?"

"Horse stepped on a rattler. Took me for a whirl."

Starkweather eyed him suspiciously.

The whole troop of men sat quiet, each taking a measure on Blake's story. Finally Starkweather asked, "So, what's going on at the neighbor's house?"

Blake looked him in the eye. It was easier now, knowing what he knew. "Nuthin," he said.

"Nothing?"

"Quiet as a tomb. They were sticking close to the house. The old man came out a couple of times. Sat on a stump of wood. The kid milked the cow. That's about it."

"No sign of guns? No sign of loading up?"

Blake shook his head.

"What about the women folk?" Jack Stone asked.

He was wearing a black suit, covered in a layer of white dust, and his duel Colts rested on his hips like cruel pet weasels. "What about that young bride? Was she about?"

This brought several hoots from the riders and Jack Stone smiled with satisfaction.

Tee Blake ignored him, still looking at Starkweather.

"Alright. Head back to the ranch. Have Cookie look at that wound. You've been up all night. You might as well get some sleep. I might send you out again tonight."

Blake nodded and slowly rode past them, knowing their eyes were on him as he passed.

"You buy it?" Jack Stone asked, once Blake was out of earshot.

"Do you?" Starkweather returned the question.

"Hell, no. That cowboy's never been thrown from a horse in his life."

Starkweather pondered this, then turned his horse away from his riders and stared thoughtfully across the sage and grass-filled plains to the distant mountains. Snow was gathering there in the higher peaks and white bands of fog hung motionless in the deeper cuts of the rim rock.

"So, Tundel isn't budging. Guess that means he'll need another nudge."

"Tonight?"

Starkweather shook his head. "No, no. Times on our side. Besides, I want Crowe out of here first. He's like a badger. Once he gets his teeth set, he's hell to shake off."

Jack Stone's brow furrowed darkly. He let his hands caress the twin pistols. "When do I get my turn?"

"Tundel is another old Yankee, just like Boone. Might be interesting to see just how far he'll go before he breaks."

"But I get the spoils?"

Starkweather nodded. "If she's still standing when this is all over."

"Oh. She'll be standing. I'll see to that."

Starkweather looked at his riders waiting patiently. He motioned to the lead rider, Ethan Moss, and waited for him to approach. "Moss. You see that snow up on those mountains."

The rider nodded, hating this condescendence.

"That snows going to be coming down on our heads in a week, maybe two."

Moss sat motionless.

"How many beeves do we have on Frenchman Pass?"

Moss closed his eyes and calculated. "Bout a thousand up there. Four times that on Melgoza Ridge. And—"

"That'll do. The Melgoza herd can wait. I'd like you to take half of these boys up to Frenchman Pass. Start bringing that herd down. It's early but there's grass down here.

"Yessir," the rider said, turning his horse.

"Wait. I'm not done. I know it's out of the way. But I want you to bring that herd down yonder." He swept his arm westward. "I think Mr. Tundel needs his garden tilled. Why not help him out by sending a thousand head through his punkin patch."

Moss sat his horse, expressionless.

"And send a rider ahead of the herd. Send that Quinn boy. Have him cut any and all wires. I don't want anything slowing these cows down once they get a pace on." He stroked his black beard, his eyes on Moss.

Jack Stone prodded his horse alongside but sat wordlessly. He too stared at the rider, watching for the least sign of discontent, but Ethan Moss wisely betrayed nothing.

"Fine then," Starkweather said. "I'll be in Dry Branch."

Jack Stone turned in his saddle. "Dry Branch? What's there?"

A smile broke through Starkweather's thick beard. "I hear they have a little saloon there. Bad whisky and warm beer. I haven't been there in over a year. Might be time to get reacquainted."

Moss lingered a moment longer then whipped his horse around and rode back to his crew. He divided them up, taking six riders with him, then without a look back they rode northward over the hill and gone.

Starkweather motioned cheerfully to the remaining riders and shouted, "Com'on boys. Let's raise a little hell."

There followed a stream of whoops and hollers and a cloud of white dust as they spurred their ponies and followed their leader down through the sage.

Fort Tillman was a fort in name only. It had once served as a wagon depot for the army, but when the army left, the name stayed. The old garrison was converted into a string of saloons, a barbershop, and a pair of mercantile. The old officers' quarters became a shabby hotel and all this was flanked by a tangle of unpainted clapboard houses and independent businesses. It was close enough to the Platte River to give it distinction, so it found its purpose as a water stop for the railroad, a watering hole for cowboys and drifters and a stopping off place for gamblers and whores. It was the whores that made it worth the ride to get there. But whores were not what Boone Crowe was looking for. His search was for a one-armed preacher.

It was midday when he entered the town under a light but steady drizzle and tied Hunter to the hitching post in front of The Commander's Saloon. Burdened by the rain, the hidden Colt under his coat, and a half-day's thirst in his throat, Boone brushed at his graying mustache and put a finger inside his cheek to pull out a wad of tobacco. He spit it into the street then beat water from his battered hat and pulled his watch from inside his vest pocket. He was not interested in the time necessarily, rather flipped the fob open and stared at a photograph framed there. He rubbed a thumb across its face with absent affection and then closed it.

Boone Crowe had only been to Fort Tillman once before, three years earlier, but by the looks of things it had doubled in size. The Commander's Saloon was new and even in midday he could hear the hollow ache of a piano jangling from deep inside. He doubted he'd find his preacher in there but it was a place to start asking questions. And a beer—he needed a beer.

For a moment he stood under the saloon's overhang, his back to the batwing doors, and gauged the immediate surroundings. Rain was dripping off the roof eaves and even in early afternoon there was a deepening grayness to the low sky. Several of the windows across the streets showed the blurred flicker of lamplight. But there were people about, mostly men, some walking in determined measure from someplace to someplace, but there were a few idlers leaning against corner posts or sitting in chairs with their feet up on a barrel, watching everything, including him. He looked at Hunter; his wet ears tilted downward, his coat slick from the rain, and at his Winchester in its sheath, and decided he'd better take the rifle with him, lest it get stolen. He didn't know this town well enough to trust anyone.

Inside The Commander's Saloon, a row of lighted wall sconces gave off a dull glow, throwing shadows onto flowered wallpaper and several gaming tables. Four men were engaged in a quiet game of cards but did not look up when Crowe entered. The long, walnut bar stretched away from him where several more men leaned over their drinks having conversation with the bartender, a thin man in a white shirt and suspenders, his hair greased with shiny tonic and combed delicately. Crowe laid his rifle on the bar and nodded to the barkeep who sauntered over and stood before him.

"What'll it be?"

Crowe pulled at his mustache again and said, "For now, a beer."

"And later?"

"I'll let you know."

The bartender stepped to a spigot and drew off a foamy beer into a big glass and returned with it. Crowe laid down some coins and looked up at the barman.

"Does the hotel have fleas?" he said.

The man laughed. "That's a good one, mister. Sorry, I can't say for sure. Depends on who slept there last, I reckon."

Boone smiled wryly. "Is there a place to sleep where I won't be pestered by the industry of women?"

The man laughed again. "You're saying you just want some sleep. That it?"

"That's it."

"Well, we get a few in here like that. Not many though." He said this with a wide smile, his temples showing a faint film of grease from his hair.

Boone Crowe drank down half of his beer in three deep swallows then wiped at the foam on his whiskers.

"Don't go next door. That's a fox den. Try The Blue Bird at the end of the street. They're reasonably clean and they serve a fair supper around six. No girls either."

"I've nothing against girls. It's just...I'm bone-weary."

From out of a dim corner a wiry fellow with a cheerful face emerged and drew near, carrying his whisky bottle and shot glass with him. He extended the bottle as a sort of offering. "Drink, mister?" The man, not young and not old, looked at the barkeep and soon another shot glass appeared before them. "You too, Sid. I'm 'bout to propose a toast and it's no fun celebrating alone."

Sid the bartender pulled a third shot glass out and the man poured whisky from his bottle into all three. "Names Corporal Larry Levinson Porter, Retired, and I lift my glass to the taming of my old friend and enemy, Sitting Bull. Drink up, men."

Crowe and Sid exchanged glances, and then together they all clicked their glasses and threw back their whisky.

"What's this about Sitting Bull?" Sid asked.

"You ain't heard then, huh."

"Heard what?"

"That old war horse finally got his fill a starvin. Come draggin down from Canady with a rag-tag band. All that's left of it anyways. Some few weeks ago I guess. Fixin to go to Fort Randall. That's the talk anyways."

He filled the glasses again. This was no news to Boone Crowe. He had received a wire from Fort Kearny concerning the business with Sitting Bull, some months, not weeks ago. He had even been invited to come to the fort and gaze upon the notorious red man, but he had declined. Still, not wanting to spoil the corporal's enthusiasm, he kept this to himself. Besides, the beer was good and the whisky, for the moment, was free.

"Ain't that something," Sid said. "He's the last of them then, ain't he?"

"With Crazy Horse dead there ain't much left."

The three men drank again.

"I fought that wily fox out in the Yellowstone," Porter said. "He was like a god to them redskins. Him and his visions. Him and his spooky old dreams. But I'd rather be his friend than his foe. Plain and simple. Wonder if he'd remember me?"

Crowe finished his whisky and returned to the rest of his beer. The card game was breaking up. One of the players stood and walked to the potbellied stove in the middle of the room and with a dirty towel that lay on the floor he opened the hot, grated door and Crowe could see the ashes glowing orange inside. The man pulled a wedge of wood from the wood box and shoved it into the stove's open mouth, then kicked the door shut again with his boot.

"How'd you hear?" Sid asked.

"Rud Lacrosse told me. He just rode in from Fort Kearny with the news."

Boone Crowe's head lifted in alarm at the name Rud Lacrosse. He drank down the last of his beer, trying not to demonstrate undo interest. Sid, unknowingly, asked the question for him.

"Where's Rud now?"

"Said he'll be around later. Maybe. Had to deliver a packet for Doc Wills first. He stunk like a hog. Wants to clean up some."

Seizing the opportunity Crowe said, "Clean up. That's a proper idea. Gents?" He lifted his empty glass. "It's been a pleasure."

Porter leaned in. "My pleasure, mister…?

He hesitated and then reluctantly said, "Crowe."

"Pleased to meet you, Mister Crowe," Porter said, extending his hand.

But Sid, under a flash of recognition, suddenly brightened. "Hell, Larry. This ain't *Mister* Crowe. This here's Marshal Crowe. Marshal Boone Crowe. Out of Buffalo. Ain't that right?"

Porter gave out a hearty laugh. "That a fact?" He stood back and looked at his guest. "Well, if this ain't a day for it. Why, you sure don't look like the old rooster-red gunfighter you're known for."

Crowe's eyes narrowed. "Rooster-red?"

"Why, folks judge you the cock-of-the-walk up in Buffalo County."

Crowe frowned. "What folks?"

"Why, most everyone left over from the old Somerset gang. The ones you didn't kill or hang."

Boone shuffled uncomfortably. "You're talking ancient history, Corporal Porter. Now, if you'll excuse me. I have a horse out front hoping for some oats and a dry bed."

Tipping his hat in Sid's direction he lifted his rifle off the bar and disappeared through the batwing doors of The Commander's Saloon in the same easy manner in which he had come in.

Ethan Moss halted his riders five miles shy of Frenchman Pass. He leaned forward and squinted into the distance, then motioned for another rider to come up.

"What is that?" Moss said, pointing to the crest of a distant hill.

"Somethin red, ain't it? Could be a boulder."

"There's no boulder there. Besides, it's too red."

"Hell, boss. It's a man. He's standing up now."

Another young rider came up pulling a small telescope from his saddlebag. "Here, Mr. Moss. Try this."

Ethan Moss pulled the brass telescope out to its full length and peered through its tiny aperture. He snorted a laugh. "Well, I'll be…its Ike Werth. And he's damn near naked."

Everyone wanted to look now, so the telescope made the rounds as the laughter picked up.

"He looks about half broke down."

"He always looks that way."

Moss shook his head. "Well, I suppose we better go rescue him. But you better stow it. Ike don't take kindly to joking."

"He ain't packin no iron," one of the riders said, still looking through the glass.

"Makes no difference. He might not be packing now—but he will be. Ike's one of Starkweather's killers from the war years. I'd rather we didn't rile him."

They all grunted their agreement then spurred their horses across the hillside toward the desperate man standing knee-deep in blue stem in his faded red long johns.

The blind Indian emerged from his shack and immediately took hold of the rope which ran from his front door to the pig pens, then, from there to the watering trough, and onward to the back door of Matt Hornfisher's livery stable. He crept along, hunched over, pulling himself along as if a sailor lost at sea, the rope acting as his lifeline, connecting him to the chores of slopping and watering the hogs. It was his way of earning the usage of the shack and for the meals that young Tanner Hornfisher brought to him every day. And it satisfied his pride. His Indian name was too long to pronounce and so had been forgotten long ago by anyone who might have shown an interest in knowing it. Some people called him Kina, mistaking him for a Canadian Indian while others called him Poncho, more out of jest than respect. But the Hornfishers called him Coyote because of how they found him, beaten and bleeding, curled up in a coyote den, nearly starved to death and half-loco.

Coyote was letting his gnarly hands slide through the rope and was nearly to the pigpen when he heard the thunder of horse's hoofs pounding the ground. They were rumbling down the main street of Dry Branch that very moment and he could feel, through the vibrating ground, that there were many of them. It caused him to bristle in terror. Without hesitation, he reversed his route and began following his guideline back to his shack. But before he reached it he could hear that a single horse had turned down the alleyway and was clomping toward him.

Coyote froze. He could feel the swirl of dust made by the horse's hooves beat against his empty eye sockets and his lips trembled. His long black hair was streaked with strands of gray and tied loosely in Indian style with a cloth band around his head, making him look like an Apache. He was old and dried from years in the sun but his red skin shown rich with the color and texture of a pomegranate. As the horse pranced around him, he turned his head away from where he believed the rider was looking.

"Well, I'll be damned," the horseman said. He drawled the words slowly, as if confounded.

Coyote did not move and the horseman did not speak again. There remained only stillness and this strange recognition that they both shared. The Indian wished the boy was here now with him. The boy would help him into his room, in his room where darkness was of a different nature than his blindness, something safer. But he had not lost everything that was Indian in him—his spirit was still intact and it could detect the evilness that filled the air around him.

At that moment Coyote felt the nudge of the boy's dog against his leg, the dog working up a deep snarl in its throat, a pot coming to boil. The rider edged closer, as if seeking a reaffirming look, his horse stomping at the ground, irritated by the growling dog. Then, after a long moment, the rider turned his horse and clomped back up the alley to the main street, leaving Coyote alone. The streets were full of horses now, the rumble of hooves filling the air, their riders raising up hoots of excitement. An occasional pistol cracked and Coyote let loose with another tremble. Finally, after he heard the clamber of boot heels on the boardwalk, his heart settled down. He turned back to the rope and began again edging toward the pigpen. It was his work. It must be done.

Ethan Moss stared down at the ox-like, scruffy gunman, his small hog's eyes set deep and brooding. The first words out of Ike Werth's mouth were, "Gimme a horse."

"Haven't a horse to spare. We're headin up to Frenchman Pass to bring the herd down. Starkweather wants it pronto."

"Gimme a horse," Ike demanded again.

"Is it safe to ask what happened to *your* horse? And...your clothes."

Ike looked at the men staring at him. If he had a gun he'd shoot them all. They had formed a circle around him and several of them looked away after spying his bare backside all red and chaffed from catching the wind. "Where is he?" Ike asked finally.

"Where is who?"

"Moss. Don't you play with me."

"If you're looking for the boss, he went into Dry Branch."

"Dry Branch? What's there?"

"I have no idea. I just follow orders. And my orders are to ride up to Frenchman and get the herd down. And that's where I'm going. You're welcome to come along if you don't mind riding double."

They stared at each other bitterly. Finally Ike said, "Gimme Pete's horse. Pete can ride double up to the herd. There'll be a horse up there for him."

Ethan Moss looked at Pete. Ike was getting agitated and they both knew it, and neither of them cared much for pressing the issue. Grudgingly, Pete climbed down from his horse and handed the reins to Ike, who wasted no time mounting and wheeling the horse around. "If I'm not at the ranch when the boss gets back tell him I rode to Fort Tillman."

"What's in Fort Tillman?"

"My horse. And the snake who stole him."

"Oh," Moss said. The riders all looked at each other and

shrugged. Then Pete flung himself up behind one of the other riders and without another word, they once again took up the trail to Frenchman Pass.

Boone Crowe found Rud Lacrosse at the Temple Saloon, sitting alone at a table in the corner eating a wedge of pumpkin pie and drinking a mug of milk. Both men had bathed and shaved and pulled on clean shirts. Lacrosse's sheepskin coat was lying across the table beside him and his hat, crown down, rested beside it. His hair was combed and his face clean and handsome. There was a thin coating of milk on Rud Lacrosse's upper lip and as Crowe approached him he pulled out his own handkerchief and handed it to the younger man.

Lacrosse looked up and then grunted a reluctant recognition. He took the outstretched handkerchief and wiped the milk from his lip. He pushed another chair out from under the table with his boot and kept eating. Crowe sat down. Neither spoke. When a girl came by Crowe ordered a beer and after a minute she brought it back and then asked Lacrosse if he wanted anything. He shook his head.

Crowe leaned back in his chair and took in the saloon. It was smaller than The Commander but more crowded. No less than three poker games were going on in varying pitch and the bar was lined with cowpunchers and townsfolk, each keeping to their own kind. He looked at Lacrosse and watched him eat, saw a light flame of premature gray at his temples. He was dressed in a black suit open at the front, a smart black vest and around his neck a large brown bandana. Crowe's own vest was tan leather and his scarf blue. On his vest, hidden by his coat, was the territorial marshal's star. Lacrosse didn't need to see it to know it was there.

"Figured you'd be east. St. Louis maybe. Or Kansas City," Crowe said. "Or in the ground," he added.

Lacrosse picked up the last piece of piecrust with his fingers and put in his mouth.

"Never heard, so that's what I figured."

Rud Lacrosse finished his milk and set the mug down heavily on the table. "If you're here to take me back, I won't go."

"Why would I want to do that?"

Lacrosse paused and their eyes met. "You know why. For dereliction of duty."

"I'm not the one who sent you. You'll have to take that up with Judge Schaffer."

They sat for a while without speaking. Finally Lacrosse asked, "So what are you doing here?"

The day was fading and from a back room appeared a young boy—a saloon acolyte—bearing a torch stick and proceeded to stand on a chair and light each wall lamp with his portable flame. It took ten minutes for the boy to complete his chores and Boone Crowe watched the whole time, sipping at his beer and gazing at the flickering glow. At last he looked back at Lacrosse and said, "The one-armed preacher. I'm looking for him."

The younger man refused to show interest. "What'd he do? Did one of his baptisms not take?"

"I want to ask him some questions. On a personal matter."

Lacrosse nodded. "I haven't seen him since I got back in town. But I'm sure he's poking around somewhere. Keeps that Indian boy with him."

"What Indian boy is that?"

"Well, he ain't a boy, really. He's a grown man now. He went away as a boy, or so I hear. He was sent to Omaha some years back. To one of those Indian schools where they cut their hair and teach them to read and write. He's back now and helps out the preacher. Doing what, I don't know."

Crowe stared solemnly at the lamp flames again and it became clear to Lacrosse that there were weighty matters on the old marshal's mind.

"You're hunting more than the preacher," he said. "You look more like the hunted than the hunter. If you don't mind me saying so."

Boone drained the last of his beer and let out a sigh, nodding thoughtfully. "I came to find out what happened to a friend of mine. They were due some time ago."

"They? Men or women?"

"What difference does it make?" The marshal answered testily.

Lacrosse shot back. "Well, I know the difference, if you don't. Besides, how's the preacher supposed to help you if you don't tell him who or what you're looking for? Hell, you might be looking for a mule for all you're saying."

Boone looked hard at Lacrosse. Finally, with an unwilling admission, he said, "*She*. She is overdue. She was supposed to be on a train to Buffalo two months ago. She stopped here to visit an old acquaintance. I've neither heard nor seen any sign of her since."

Lacrosse smiled mildly. "Why're you so cranky?"

Boone Crowe put his fingers in his empty beer glass and spun it around like a child playing with a top. "I'm a private man," was all he said, not looking up.

"Who was she here to visit?"

"I don't know that. She never said."

"That's not very helpful."

"I thought the preacher might know of her."

"He might," said Lacrosse. He looked at the old marshal, at his battered black hat, at the graying mustache, the deep-set eyes, and saw the pain of an unsolved mystery working his troubled face.

A poker player at a nearby table suddenly leapt up and let out a string of oaths. The crowd turned and stared at him. The poker player's feet were set and the chair behind him tipped, on the verge of toppling onto the floor. The four or five other players scattered, leaving one lone man still in his seat. Eventually the chair did hit the floor, sending up a clatter that added to the tension. The lone poker player remained sitting, unfettered, and coolly collecting his chips. The cursing player rubbed the palm of his right hand against his shirt, as if drying off sweat. His holster was empty but his pistol lay on the poker table and his eyes were focusing on it.

"That'll do," thundered the barkeep from a dark corner of the saloon. He stood there, a double-barreled shotgun resting in the crook of his arm, leveled at the unhappy card player. "There won't be any of that in here. Take what's yours and get out."

"That man is a cheat."

"I said, get what belongs to you and get out."

The poker player fidgeted. "That pistol is mine."

The barkeep shook his head. "Leave it where it lays. You can pick it up later at the sheriff's office."

Boone Crowe and Rud Lacrosse watched the barkeep with peculiar admiration. There was a further moment of anxious silence. The entire saloon, the people in it, and even the structure itself, seemed to hold its collective breath. Finally the man backed away from the table, almost stumbling on the chair behind him. He threw one last glance at the pistol on the table, then turned and taking long strides, left the saloon, letting the batwings flap in his wake.

"Smart man," Crowe said, as the atmosphere settled down. But glancing at Lacrosse he saw an expression of fury in his face. "You okay?"

Lacrosse stood up from his chair and was reaching for his sheepskin coat still lying on the table when the batwings burst apart again. The angry gambler had returned. He came so fast he appeared as a blur and from his hand burst a loud roar and an orange flame that flashed nearly in Boone's turned face. In the next half-second the cool poker player, still sitting behind his pile of winnings, was thrown violently against the wall, a splash of blood across his chest.

Then, without pause, Lacrosse, still reaching for his coat, produced a pistol from beneath its folds and without hesitation fired a shot that tore through the unhappy gambler's throat and thrust him dead on the floor.

The air seemed to rush out of the place then, as if in a vacuum. Though these men were not unaccustomed to violence, the crowd stood dumb in unsettled alarm. Even Crowe, one arm still halfway inside his own coat, reaching for his hidden Colt, gaped in wonder at what had just happened. Gun smoke drifted listlessly around the room as Rud Lacrosse slowly let his arm settle down at his side, a mild shaking in the tight fist that gripped the pistol.

The barkeep came around from behind the bar, his shotgun still in his hand. He walked over and stood above the dead shooter, followed by several others. "Who was that fellow?" he asked. "Anybody know?"

For a while no one spoke. Finally a young wrangler stepped forward. "Can't rightly fetch his name to mind. But he rides for Starkweather. That much I know."

As if his head was operating on a mechanical turret, Boone Crowe slowly rotated his neck until his eyes fell on Lacrosse. The younger man's face was still aflame with fury. "We need to talk," Crowe said.

Chapter 4

OLD MAN TUNDEL stood over the freshly turned earth that covered his son. The rest of the family had returned to the house, leaving him alone beside the grave. His wife had wept out a few words of scripture—*Oh, that I had wings like a dove! For then would I fly away and be at rest*—and Lucy had laid a hand-woven wreath of late squash blossoms next to the hastily etched, wooden marker: Junson Tundel. Passed 1881. But the sad service, and the filling of the hole with the silent toil of shovels, took less than a quarter of an hour.

The talk around the table that morning, after a night of sleepless sorrow, had been bitter. Only during the burial itself had the grievous disagreements of the family finally been silenced. Now though, and even from this distance, he could hear again the blustering echo of Virgil's agitated voice, as it seemed to beat against the windowpanes of the house.

Ernest Tundel's gaze flared northward, through the canyon bottom, in the direction of his two recently burnt out neighbors. The Hamms went first, eight months ago. Chester Hamm had been absent that March evening but his brother, Lance, told him how eight or ten riders had rode in and torched the barn. Lance emptied his Winchester at them from the house, hitting one rider, but received two wounds for his trouble, one to his shoulder and the other tearing into his chest. He lay near death in the dooryard and watched hopelessly as the riders—masked as they were—throwing their torches onto the roof of the house. Lance dragged himself as best he could away from the heat of the flames. When Chester returned, he found his brother where he lay, with only enough life left in him to give witness to the tragedy.

The shot rider was dead but Chester Hamm knew he was no cowpuncher, rather one of the big cattleman's watchdog regulators. He buried his brother in a deep grave and then stripping the dead rider, hoisted the naked body into the pigpen, where the hogs, already wild with the smell of blood, made quick work of him. It was the only justice he had left. The law was sent for and word was that Judge Schaffer was going to send a deputy marshal down to investigate, but he was never seen.

Bad as that was, the burning out of the Woodson's was worse. John and his wife, Resty, were both home, as was their fourteen-year-old daughter, Elizabeth. There were no witnesses to this, but it followed in the same pattern as the Hamm homestead, with one hideous exception—both women had been violated. John's charred body was found inside the boundary of the burnt barn, but the grounds outside the house showed signs of a great struggle. Both mother and daughter were found unburnt but scratched and beaten to the brink of torture. Ernest Tundel saw the smoke early the next morning and he and Virgil had ridden over to investigate and found both Resty and Elizabeth dead. They showed no signs of having been shot but had clearly been left to die by their tormenter. The raiders' trail disappeared into the hardpan but a single rider had branched off and it appeared, for a while at least, that this lone rider was following someone. A horseless someone. Ernest and Virgil followed the tracks to the creek, but it was running high and they never did find an emerging trail.

The Tundels would be next. Ernest knew it. And Virgil knew it. The whole family knew it. Once, after Hamm was run off, the old man decided to go directly at Starkweather. He tried to gather a vigilance posse, but when the Woodson thing occurred, no one had the stomach to take on the cattleman. Now Judson was dead. The first blow had been struck, and it was a blow so severe, and so well placed, that now Ernest Tundel could be numbered among the afraid. In the war he had faced horror upon horror, but then, it was just he alone. No wife or children to fret over. This was different. And the visit yesterday of Marshal Boone Crowe gave him little if any comfort. Help had not come before; surely it would not come now. And the sight of those two dead women haunted him still.

Starkweather's cowboys found the whisky in Clive Leyland's tiny saloon adequate for the purpose. It wiped away the dust of the trail, and in time scrubbed clean their memories of past deeds. They fell to playing cards in a dark corner, rolled cigarettes hanging from their bottom lips, their spurs gouging at the chair legs. Two of the boys circled the pool table clumsily, while another pair threw darts at a bull's-eye attached to the wall, missing more times that hitting. Starkweather and Jack Stone leaned at the bar trying to draw the disinclined Leyland into conversation.

"You could use a little more light in here," Starkweather said. "Man likes to see what he's got in his hand. What if he raised the table thinking he had a flush, when all he had was a pair of deuces?"

"That would be a crime," said Jack Stone.

"Could lead to trouble," Starkweather agreed.

Leyland stood his distance, running a rag across a row of glasses.

"If this was my place," Jack Stone said, "I'd put another window in. Right there." He whipped one of his pistols out and pointed it toward the wall near the door. "Right there," he said again.

Leyland waited for the dark man to shoot a hole in the wall but nothing happened. Stone twirled his pistol then returned it to its holster.

"Mooorre whisky," shouted one of the card players. "More whissk—" Before he could finish his sentence he fell out of his chair, hitting the floor with a thud. Another cowpuncher stood up and walked over to his fallen companion, examining him.

"Shorty's out."

He picked up Shorty's cards and threw them on the table. "Too bad," said another. "He had four of a kind." This brought a wild round of laughter from the others.

"Give 'em another bottle, Leyland," Starkweather commanded. "You're making money today."

Leyland threw down the rag and snatched another bottle

from the shelf and walked it over to the card table. One of the cowboys grabbed for it but lost it in his drunken grip and the bottle fell to the floor, rolling under the table. The cowboy immediately stood up and made a stab for his holster. The rest of the card players scattered.

"Watch out, Pat."

But Pat had finally gotten a sloppy grip on his pistol and proceeded to fire at the rolling bottle. "Look out, or it'll bite ye," he shouted jovially.

Starkweather and Jack Stone turned and watched the havoc, grinning. Meanwhile, Pat had emptied his pistol into the floor without hitting the bottle. It rolled onward, heading for the corner, by which time two other punchers had their pistols out and were filling the floor with lead. Suddenly, in a blur, Jack Stone had both Colts out and in a roaring barrage of bullets he reduced the whisky bottle into a flying eddy of glass chards. Before Leyland had a chance to focus, Jack Stone's pistols were back in their sheaths.

Blue gun smoke hung heavy in the room. A cowboy whistled in admiration. The two pool players stood dumbly, holding their cue sticks as if they were fishing poles.

"Nice piece of shooting," Starkweather said. He turned. "Don't you think so, Mr. Leyland?"

Clive Leyland said nothing.

"I asked you a question. Did you like that shooting?"

Leyland felt his fingers twitching. He shook his head haltingly. "I…I did not like it. You have made a mess of…of my place."

Starkweather stroked his beard. He turned to Jack Stone.

"Mr. Leyland here is not an appreciator of your talent. Perhaps it was because it happened so fast he couldn't see it." He motioned for one of the dart throwers to fetch another whisky bottle.

"You want I should put it on the table, boss."

"No, A. J. Just hold it."

The cowboy A. J. shuddered, looking at the bottle as if it were a snake. "Wha…what fer…"

Jack Stone's Colts came up again and instantly two bullets exploded the bottle, leaving a shaken A. J. holding only the neck, the front of his shirt covered in glass and whisky.

"Did you see it that time, Mr. Leyland?" Starkweather asked.

Leyland's face was crimson. Through the batwings he could see where Amos had come to find out what the shooting was about. Behind him was Matthew Hornfisher. Leyland shook his head in their direction, indicating for them to go away, that it wasn't safe. After a moment their faces disappeared.

"I'm waiting, Leyland. Or do you need another demonstration?"

Leyland swallowed back his fear. "I need nothing more. I have seen it. Now please. No more shooting."

The cowboys, drunk as they were, let their eyes pass between the two men, knowing from past experiences the direction this evening could take. They watched silently, not wanting to have anything to do with Jack Stone or his pistols. A. J., still clutching the bottleneck, had turned pale as cake flour.

"Leyland. I happen to be a gentleman of Southern gentry. And to your credit, you have said 'please'. In Mississippi, that is a word to be honored. I will thank you for your hospitality and send these cow handlers back to their accustomed barracks. Men!" He turned to his riders and motioned for the door, by which, somewhat relieved themselves, they gathered up their things and stumbled out to their horses.

Jack Stone smiled his black smile.

Finally, Starkweather picked up his unfinished glass of whisky and slowly drank it down, wiping his beard with his gloved hand. "One thing more, Leyland," he said, stepping close. "Next time we come into Dry Branch I hope to find another window in that wall over there."

"And some women," sneered Jack Stone. "We need some pretty gals to dance with."

Leyland stood in sober silence.

The cattleman reached into his long gray coat and then slapped down a handful of silver onto the bar. "I could not tolerate it if word got around that Captain Douglas Starkweather did not pay his debts."

Jack Stone leered. "You ought to nail down some bean can lids over them holes in the floor. Winters coming. You wouldn't want any rats in here, would you?"

It was Leyland's thought, at that moment, as the Starkweather band rode out of Dry Branch with hoots and wild gunshots that the worst of all rats had just departed.

Ten miles to the northwest, at the Ashmun ranch, Freya Ashmun moved through the parlor of the ranch house with a long matchstick holding it to the wicks of candles. Yuridia, the Ashmun's young domestic, on her hands and knees, busied herself at the face of the broad fireplace, coaxing a flame into life. Freya's father was still with the roundup so she had the evening—and the house—to herself.

"Deed you eat, Señorita?"

Freya shook her head. "Don't bother tonight, Yuridia. Food is the furthest thing from my thoughts. I just want to sit quietly."

"I am sorry for you friend."

"You heard, then?"

"Leetle George tol' one of Señor Ashmun's riders. He bring me the word."

Freya pressed her teeth against her lip to keep them from quivering. The two women's eyes met and the gentle Yuridia nodded solemnly.

After a time Freya thanked the Mexican girl, then excused her for the rest of the evening. "The fire is nice. I'll just relax here for a while."

The big house seemed uncharacteristically quiet, so often otherwise filled with the heavy boot steps and booming commands of Ward Ashmun. Though it housed only father and daughter, along with Yuridia, it seemed more like an army barracks than a private residence, and the parlor more like a war room where noisy conferences were held between

Ashmun, the foreman Wes Bridges, and the lead riders. Ward Ashmun's raucous, thickly accented orders left little room for compromise. He was one of a number of Englishman who had left the distant isle to settle in the American west, and with him came the attitude of monarch-like dominion. Already bred with an air of superiority, Ashmun did not hide his disdain for squatters and farmers. He hated anything that had to do with wire fences or the sodbusters that came with it. Still, he neither harbored any respect for Douglas Starkweather, or that man's methods for driving the settlers away with violence. To him, Starkweather was nothing less than an assassin, who surrounded himself with cutthroats left over from the American war. The only good thing about Ernest Tundel, Ashmun was once heard to say, was that Tundel's little homestead marked a convenient line of separation between the Ashmun spread and Starkweather's. But his daughter's friendship with Junson Tundel was taking that generosity too far.

Freya watched the fire widen in the grate then went and stood before a row of books above the mantle. She had spent barely fourteen months at a school in the east when her mother took ill. She arrived back in Wyoming only in time to see her die. That was years ago. Books had been a way for her mother to fight the long hours of boredom living in a big house on a big range in a wide and sometimes terrible land. Books had been her deepest pleasure and she often had them sent to her from as far away as England. Touching the cold spines now, Freya saw *The Hand of Ethelberta* by Thomas

Hardy, which had reminded her mother of the old English villages. Another favorite was an ancient copy of *John Scott of Amwell,* the Quaker poet of Hertfordshire. It was this volume she pulled from the shelf now, blowing dust from the dull pages.

Moving to a big horsehair chair, she sat and opened to a familiar page, a page marked with a scrap of cloth. She knew many of the poems by heart, for they had been read to her as a child, and even now, as she scanned the page, it was her mother's voice she heard, not her own—

I hate that drum's discordant sound
Parading round, and round, and round;
To me it talks of ravag'd plains,
And burning towns, and ruin'd swains,
And mangled limbs, and dying groans,
And widow's tears, and orphans' moans;
And all that Misery's hand bestows.

It was Junson Tundel she saw in the middle of these lines. His mangled limbs and dying groans. It was these ravaged Wyoming plains. It was Starkweather, and the towns and places it was rumored he had burned. It was the people and all this…

She stopped suddenly, sucking in a breath. Outside, on the hard packed ground of the yard, she could hear the approaching clop of a horse's hooves. It was late and the barns and corrals stood silent in the evening darkness. The bunkhouse was empty as all the riders were at the roundup. And surely her father had not ridden back early. He would never do that. She sat still and listened as the hoof beats drew closer. Yuridia had heard them too and had come to the stairway landing. Freya looked up at her, but neither girl spoke. Finally, the horse stopped and a long minute passed before a spurred boot hit the first step of the porch with a thud and a jingle. Slowly the heavy steps came all the way to the door and at last Freya rose from her chair and stood, waiting. A knocked sounded.

"Who—" Her voice cracked. Had Bridges come back? No. He would have announced himself long ago. "Who is it?"

"It's late, I know. I was hopin to speak to Mr. Ashmun."

Alarm was suddenly replaced by anger. Freya felt her small hands pull themselves into fists. She looked once more at Yuridia then stomped to the door and with a determined heave, pulled it open.

In the dim light of a porch lamp, Freya found herself standing face to face with a young cowboy, his plaid shirt clean but wrinkled, his face shaved and his sandy hair plastered flat on his head, chaps weathered and his hat in his hand. There was an odd crease of raw red skin at his scalp.

"What do you want," she said, hotly.

Eyes cast downward, the cowboy said, "Pardon the interruption. I rode all day to get here. I was wantin to see Mr. Ashmun."

"About what?"

He raised his head then and looked around. Over Freya's shoulder, in the flicker of fireplace light, he could see a young Mexican girl standing on the last step of a stairway, the barrel of a shotgun tilted in his direction. "Maybe I ought to leave. I could come back in the morning." He took a step back.

"Who are you and what do you want?"

He fidgeted, his boots scraping the wood planks. "I was hopin Mr. Ashmun might need another hand."

Freya felt brave. "He is not here. He is up at the roundup. And I do not know if he needs another rider or not. What is your name?"

The cowboy swallowed. "Names Blake, ma'am. Tee Blake they call me."

"Well, Mister Tee Blake. I saw you before. I saw you in Dry Branch. You are a Starkweather rider. And Starkweather riders are not welcome here." She grabbed the door and with a mighty force slammed it in the cowboy's face.

"Miss Ashmun," he said, his voice muffled by the door. "I no longer ride for Starkweather. I quit him this morning."

A long pause followed, and then the cowboy's boots could be heard descending the steps. In another moment the shuffle of his horse's hoofs rang dully in the yard. Then the door was flung open again and Freya stepped onto the porch.

"Why did you quit him," she hollered.

Blake pulled up his horse and walked it slowly toward the house where they were washed in moonlight. He took his hat off again while addressing her. "Cowhands don't get paid much, Miss Ashmun. But a cowhand is what I am. Starkweather is something else. He wants things from me I can't give him."

The sheriff of Fort Tillman, Carl Hoody, sat on the corner of his worn oak desk and looked at the two men in front of him. Crowe was sitting in a chair, tilting it back on its hind legs, boots crossed at the ankles in front of him, his fingers tapping on the wooden armrests in some incomprehensible rhythm. Lacrosse stood in a corner, occasionally pacing to the window and gazing out at nothing in particular.

"Did you know this was a Starkweather man before you shot him," asked the sheriff, a thin, unassuming man with a drawn face and dull eyes.

"I—"

Crowe interrupted. "What difference does that make? It was a snap decision. And he did the right thing."

"It might make a difference to Starkweather. I talked to everyone in the saloon. Lacrosse here did the right thing. No question. But I want to know."

"I think you're prying under the wrong rock, sheriff."

"And I think you ought to let Rud answer. There's things afoot here that apparently you know nothing about, marshal."

Crowe shot a glance at Lacrosse. "Like what? What don't I know?"

"Rud? You want to tell him? It might settle a lot."

Crowe stood from his chair. "Will you two stop playing games and get on with it?"

Lacrosse turned from the window and faced the marshal. With his left hand he reached up and gripped the wide, brown scarf above his collar. Pulling the cloth down and twisting his head to the side, he revealed the broad path of a hideous, coarse scar ringing his neck. Lacrosse held it there, the ugly disfigurement red against the tan of his skin.

Boone Crowe recoiled in alarm. "What the—"

"They hung him," the sheriff said. "Or they tried."

"Who hung him?"

"Starkweather. And his men."

Crowe looked at Lacrosse, who was refashioning his scarf to hide the mark.

"What the hell happened?"

Lacrosse looked at the sheriff. "That man." He tilted his head in the direction of the saloon. "His name was Clemons. He was one of them holding the rope. I recognized him when he stood up, making that ruckus."

"He held the rope."

Lacrosse nodded. "He and another jackal. Judge Schaffer's only instruction to me was to just snoop around. There'd been rumors that folks had been having trouble and that this fellow Starkweather was behind some of their unhappiness. There had been a place burned out. And a killing. I was to investigate. I don't think the judge put much stock in it."

"Who was killed," Crowe asked.

"Farmer named Hamm. I talked to his brother, who was just packing up to head back to Missouri. He said his dying brother implicated Starkweather's men."

"So you headed to Starkweather."

"I didn't get far. His men watch everything. That range is like a fishbowl. Nothing coming or going gets unnoticed. They watched me leave the Hamm place. Or what was left of it. Nothing but burnt timbers and dead animals."

"And?"

"Hamm told me I ought to check in with his neighbors first. Make sure they were well-warned."

"Was one of them neighbors Tundel?"

"Seems it was. Said the Tundels had come to help quick as they spied smoke but it was too late. How do you know them Tundel folks?"

Boone Crowe told Lacrosse and the sheriff about his run-in with Brady Quinn in Dry Branch, about the death of Junson Tundel, and about killing one of Starkweather's idiot gunslingers right on Starkweather's range."

The sheriff turned away, shaking his head dismally.

"Tell me about the hanging."

"Not much to tell. His riders cornered me in a gulch right under a big old tree. They saw the badge and it set em off. 'We're the law around here' one of them said. 'This is Starkweather land and the law ain't welcome.' I told them to move aside and let me do my work. It was a bad bluff. Out came the rope."

"And they strung you up? Just like that?"

"Not exactly. They wanted some sport first. They lassoed me off my horse. Then they disarmed me. One of them put the rope around my neck. And then that man Clemons threw the loose end up over a branch. And then he begins giving it sharp yanks."

The sheriff turned around and he and Crowe's eyes met. They both looked at Lacrosse and saw that he was no longer there with them; rather he was back on that range, standing under that tree, his eyes ablaze with anger and fear.

"They pulled me off the ground and let me swing. Then they'd let me drop. Then up again. Longer each time. When they'd let me back down I could hear them laughing. All this time one man was giving a speech. A man dressed in black. He was talking about the war. Rambling on and on about it."

"Starkweather," the sheriff said.

Lacrosse shook his head.

"Jack Stone, then." Crowe said. "Starkweather's chief pirate."

"Starkweather was up on the hill, sitting his horse," Lacrosse continued. "He was watching everything. I was pretty much spent. They had let me hang once for near a minute. When they finally let me drop I heard grumbling. Some of the men wanted to finish the job. Lying there on the ground I could just see Starkweather wave his arm from the hilltop, his signal that it was over."

Lacrosse moved back to the window. After a moment Crowe said, "Over. Until tonight."

Just as twilight blanketed the street with a pink dust, Ike Werth ambled into Fort Tillman on a worn down horse that was not his own. Passing the undertaker's office his gaze fell upon two simple pine caskets, each propped up against the wall, the lids off, the deceased occupants looking restful if not satisfied. He plodded to that side of the street and peering through the fading light on their faces he was shocked to see someone who looked like Milo Clemons. He sat in his saddle staring, then finally dismounted and stepped onto the boardwalk for a closer look.

It *was* Clemons. *Now what did he do to get himself killed like that*? he wondered. He glanced at the other dead man, who he did not know, and supposed they had killed each other. Studying Clemons more closely, he saw that he was in a bad way, his throat torn apart, and the biggest share of his left temple blown to pieces. His partner in death showed only a neat bullet hole in his checkered vest.

Ike turned from the corpses. Death held no surprise for him. The war had hardened him beyond repair. After that he saw death—and even killing—as the simple slaughter of another barnyard animal. He had left his soul at Cold Harbor in 1864. From there it was nothing but a killing field, even into Texas and Mexico, against the Apache, the greasers, the carpetbaggers, and anything that got in their way. When Shelby went soft and headed back to the states, Starkweather and Stone drove deeper into the mesquite country, killing Frenchmen for Benito Juarez. They took Ike and Clemons with them and they had been with them ever since. Except now Clemons was finished.

This will not be pleasing news for Starkweather.

Leyland, Amos, and Matthew Hornfisher sat into the late night drinking hot coffee and speculating on the strange events of the day. Starkweather, they knew, was a man who took pleasure in surprises. It was clear, from past experiences that the cattleman was a calculating villain, whose every move was to shock or intimidate. On this day he had accomplished both.

"He hasn't been around here for months," Amos said. "Why now? What's he want with us?"

"He's after Tundel," Hornfisher said. "And he wants to make sure nobody in Dry Branch gets in the way."

Leyland nodded in agreement. "He turned that kid loose on Junson. That killing was a message. Plain as if it was writ out."

They had been around to this conclusion several times already this night, and each time they ended it by staring into their coffee mugs, wishing they were wrong, each remembering the murdered Tundel boy in the street. It *was* murder and they all knew it. But who was going to stand up and call out Starkweather.

"Lot of good that marshal was," Amos said. "He lit out like an antelope."

"Maybe," said Hornfisher, thoughtfully. "Little George got an earful from some range rider. Said the marshal rode right onto Starkweather's spread yesterday morning. The range rider told LG there was some gun play and that the marshal put one of Starkweather's men under."

Leyland and Amos exchanged skeptical glances. "And Boone Crowe ain't dead?"

"Don't know any more. LG said the rider got the story from one of Starkweather's men. Someone he's sort of friendly with."

"Who was it got killed?"

"Didn't say."

Clive Leyland shook his head. "I think Little George must have dreamt it."

"I doubt Marshal Crowe even got close to Starkweather's place," Amos agreed. "And if he did, he musta been lost. That place is fortified better then old Fort Laramie in its day."

Matthew Hornfisher lifted his coffee mug then put it back down without taking a drink. "Say what you will. But LG gives better news than the *Cheyenne Gazette*."

Ethan Moss and the rest of Starkweather's riders reached the range at Frenchman Pass well after dark. They caught Brady Quinn just as he was about to ride out for his turn at night watch.

"Might as well pack it up, Quinn," Moss said. "Boss has a special job for you."

Quinn coaxed his horse alongside Moss and the two men searched for each other's faces in the shadows. It was a well-established truth that neither liked the other. Moss was a cowboy, a proven foreman, while Brady Quinn was what

Moss called a brush puppy, a wet-behind-the-ears tramp that had sidled up to Starkweather's good side by being an overeager errand boy. Now, word was, Quinn was a killer too.

"We're to move this herd down startin tomorrow. Soon as we get em together."

"Yeah. What's my job?" Quinn asked.

"Boss wants you to ride ahead of the herd and cut any wire that might hinder the drive."

"There ain't no wire on our range."

"We ain't drivin them that way. Boss wants us to run em through Tundel's spread. Give his corn some cultivatin."

Brady smiled. "Well, that's a job for me," he said, cheerfully.

"Pete'll take your watch. You can head out right away. We'll bring down your kit when we come."

"Yaahoo," Quinn hollered. "Ain't life grand?"

"You got a wire cutter?"

Quinn patted his saddlebag.

"Then get going. Boss'll want to know how it goes."

Cutting his horse toward the trail, Brady let out another whoop and rode off into the night. Moss watched him go and thought how fine it would be if one of the Tundels put Brady Quinn in their sights and blew the little cocksure fool to kingdom come.

Brady Quinn rode with the devil at his heels. Into the

Wyoming darkness he plunged, a slow rising moon throwing a silver shadow over the range. He knew the lay of the land leading up to the Tundel spread from his many scouting trips under Starkweather's orders. In fact, he knew a great deal about these rouge settlements. He had been present at both the Hamm and the Woodson burnouts. In fact it may well have been a shot from his own pistol that had dropped Lance Hamm in his doorway. There was no proof, of course. There was shooting all around. But he had certainly been aiming his shots at the old man, who had stood in the fiery outline of his blazing yard.

The Woodsons had been different though. Only one shot had been fired. The one that dropped Woodson. That had been Ike's shot. Once the three women were brought into the yard, Mr. Starkweather ordered most of us back. He left Milo Clemons and Jack Stone to take care of them. Brady had hung back, concealed by the smoke of the burning barn, and watched as Jack Stone wrestled the little girl around by her hair, throwing her to the ground. The mother screamed and tried to fight him off but Jack Stone simply knocked her to the ground with a backhanded cuff.

And then there was the third woman.

Even as the mother was back on her feet, trying mightily to get between Jack Stone and her daughter—the girl's clothes already torn mostly off—the mother was yelling for this third woman to run. In the crashing of barn timbers, above the roar of the flames, and even beyond the screaming of the girl, the words found Quinn's ears—*Run, Eva! Run…Eva…*

And for a moment it seemed as if, in her fear and confusion, this woman was about to flee straight into Quinn's very grasp. Her nightgown flashed white against the black night, coming directly toward him, her head tossing in wild fright. Suddenly, one whole side of the barn collapsed in a flurry of flying sparks and flaming chards of wood. It was all Quinn could do to spur his horse out of the way. But when he regained himself, the woman was gone.

By this time, Jack Stone dragged both mother and daughter back into the house and all that remained was Clemons' account the next morning of what had happened. It left Brady Quinn with a mixture of thrill and dread. It took a strange and potent man to fear nothing. Jack Stone was that man. He feared neither God nor the devil. Perhaps Jack Stone *was* the devil. Regardless, Brady Quinn had only two thoughts concerning Jack Stone—either stay far out of his way, or be the man who killed him.

This last thought is what thrilled him.

Virgil and Lucy Tundel stood facing each other in their quarters of the house. It was late but neither had prepared for bed. In fact, Virgil had just then laid his coat across a chair and went back to running a cleaning rod down the barrel of the Sharps. He was going out again.

"But your father—"

"Forget Pa. He and I don't agree. That's plain."

"He's trying to do what's right."

Virgil ignored her, sliding the rod back out and then leaning it in a corner. He lifted a bandoleer from a wooden peg and hoisted it over his head and onto his shoulder. As he reached for his coat she grabbed his hand but he shook it off.

"Virgil," she said, her voice sharp. "What good will you be to me if you are dead? What good will you be to any of us?"

He looked at her but her beauty was a distraction to his anger so he turned away. "I never thought Pa would be someone to cut and run."

"He never said that. He—"

"Lucy! I will not sit here and let them come for us. That's what Pa wants. But it's not what I want."

"What about what I want? Do I not account for anything?"

"Not when it comes to this. Starkweather needs to be hurt. Tonight I will get him where it will hurt."

"Have you forgotten what happened to the Woodsons?"

"How could I? Why do you think I need to do this?"

"Oh! To abandon me at a time when I need your protection the most."

Virgil turned now finally and faced her. There was fire in his eyes. "Woman, I have heard enough. You have Pa to protect you."

"You just said your father was afraid."

"Fine then." He grabbed his Sharps by the barrel and stepped to the door, bumping her out of his way. He turned and glared at her with bitterness. "Fine," he said again.

"Then you can get August to protect you."

She did not flinch from this last insult, only watched him disappear into the night.

Ike Werth found his horse in a back stall of the dimly lit livery stable. He'd found the marshal's horse too, a sleek animal that Ike coveted. He had watched from an alley as the livery caretaker had crossed the street to fetch his supper, and then entered through an open back door. The marshal's horse was fidgety at his presence, so, enveloped in darkness, he collapsed on a pile of straw across in a facing stall.

A grandstand seat, Ike thought. It may be a while, but that damned marshal will eventually be back. "I'll just sit tight," he whispered. But after a half hour he wished he had bought himself a bottle at the saloon. It might be a long cold night.

An hour later he was startled out of his sleep by the returning liveryman. "Hey. You there. What're you doin in here?"

"Huh! What—" Ike fumbled for his pistol. He had laid it across his lap so that it would be handy, but in his unplanned slumber it had fallen into the straw at his side. Still groggy, he groped for it clumsily, keeping one eye on the shadowy form before him.

"State yer business, mister," the liveryman called out, even as he began backing away, sensing trouble.

Ike's brain was fogged from a full forty-eight hours without sleep. Finally lumbering onto his knees he used both hands to rummage the straw. He found the pistol, but in his awkward state one of his fingers slipped into the trigger guard and pulled the trigger, sending a loud shot into the dirt in front of him.

At this the liveryman bolted, running down the street and hollering for Sheriff Hoody.

Ike cursed himself to his feet. Holstering his pistol he stood stupidly in the dark for a moment trying to calculate his next move. All surprise was gone now. Best to hightail it, he guessed.

The gunshot had spooked the horses and as he moved in their midst, Hunter lifted a knowing hind leg and with lightning speed struck out, his sharp hoof hitting Ike Werth on the side of the head. Lifted off his feet, he settled senselessly onto the dusty, straw-strewn floor of the livery.

The gunshot raised little alarm in Fort Tillman, but the liveryman's hollering did. In haste the lawmen followed the liveryman back to the barn where they found the sprawled gunman.

"Is he dead?"

"Depends on what you mean by dead," Hoody said, holding his ear close to Ike's lips, checking for breathing. He turned and motioned to the liveryman. "Newt. Run. Get Doc Wills. If he ain't dead now, he'll be wishing he was."

Lacrosse stood back, watching Marshal Boone Crowe inspecting the hind hooves of Hunter. Crowe wouldn't be surprised to see blood on the horseshoe and as it was, there shown a fresh swath of muddy dirt clotted on the iron. He dabbed at it, rubbing it between his fingers. He let go of Hunter's hoof and patted him lovingly on his flanks.

"You know this feller?" Hoody asked.

Both Crowe and Lacrosse said yes.

The sheriff looked up at Lacrosse. "You too, huh? He one of them that hung you?"

Lacrosse nodded solemnly.

"I should have killed him yesterday," Crowe joined in. "I left him afoot after he tried to dry-gulch me. That's his horse stalled over there."

They stood around with no further words until Newt came back with Doc Wills in tow. The doorway had clogged with a half dozen curiosity-seekers drawn by the commotion.

The doctor bent down and ran a quick examination. "Newt," he said. "For crying out loud, get some light over here."

Newt sprang forth with a lantern and held it above Ike's dented head.

"Horse do this?" It was a pointless question, so no one answered. "Well, let's get him up to my office." He turned to the doorway and to the men peering in. "Com'on you pack of jackdaws. Get in here and lend a hand."

The three lawmen watched as Ike Werth was carted out in the arms of four townsmen. Finally Sheriff Hoody said, "He was layin for somebody."

"He was layin for me," Crowe answered.

Hoody looked at Lacrosse and then back to Boone

Crowe. "This hasn't been a very good day for Starkweather."

Tee Blake erected a loose-fitted windbreak in a grove of trees a mile above the Ashmun ranch. From here he could faintly make out the dim flicker of lights from Ashmun's house. He gathered the makings for a small fire and once it was going he warmed himself against the growing cold. He pulled at a hard biscuit and washed it down with swigs from his canteen. The picture of the girl was still in his head. Her face, and the face of the Mexican girl. The one holding the shotgun. Trouble was not what he was looking for. Trouble was what he had just left. What he wanted was a job. But now he had his doubts. Maybe he should just keep riding. Somewhere further north. Leaving Starkweather like he did could make me a marked man, he reasoned. And riding for the opposition would only make it worse.

My father is up at the roundup. I don't know when he'll return. And I doubt that he would hire you anyway.

He fell asleep curled in his blankets.

Sometime in the middle of the night he woke to the sound of hoof beats. His fire was dead but against the moon, a thousand yards away, he saw the silhouette of a single horseman riding with intent, the long black spear of a rifle barrel extending from his free hand.

Virgil Tundel hoped he was leaving a clear trail. He left Lucy standing in the dark doorway and had lit out straight for one of Ward Ashmun's several horse corrals. He had laid out his plan even as they were throwing dirt on Junson's casket. Keeping to a vein of bedrock in order to not leave any distinguishable tracks, he tied his mount in a well-concealed ravine and crept up and over the next rise until he reached the watering hole and the rail corral. The horses were part of a spare remuda that Ashmun held in reserve for when he had to hire a cluster of riders for driving big herds to the railheads. In a makeshift lean-to built onto the base of the windmill, he found saddles and bridles covered with tarps.

Within minutes he had cut a fleet-footed gelding from the herd and once saddled was galloping across the range in the direction of Starkweather's Melgoza pastures leaving deep hoof prints in the soft grassland. Melgoza was the closest of Starkweather's herds and Virgil knew he would find both cattle and cowboys up there. By midnight he started seeing cows strung loosely along the hillsides and as he kept riding he found himself moving closer to the main body of the herd. Here he dismounted and tying his horse out of sight, he found a forked sapling where he could steady the barrel of his Sharps. Then slowly and methodically he began shooting Starkweather's cows. The cattle fell stupidly at first, the way he had heard the bison once did, showing little alarm at the gunfire.

After he had killed eight prime beeves, he paused and waited. The cattle now were stirring and finally, just as he had hoped, the shadow of a rider broke the plain of the hillside. It was a fifty-yard shot but Virgil lifted the rider out of his saddle with a single squeeze of the trigger. The sound of another horseman came galloping from the opposite direction. Virgil aimed at the dark blur and shot again and he could hear the cry of a man and the sharp whine of the horse.

The herd was panicked now. Firing once more in the air, Virgil attempted to drive the herd in the direction of the second fallen rider, hoping the stampede would finish the job in the event he had missed. He quickly regained his horse, and loading his Sharps one last time he shot into the tail end of the herd, dropping another steer. Then it was off to the races, galloping hard down the same path he had come up on. He wanted his trail to be easy to follow—straight to Ashmun's.

By the time Virgil reached the corrals the horse was lathered and winded. He did not remove the saddle, simply opened the gate and shooed it back in. Dawn's first pink blade was cutting the horizon as he rode his horse back across the rim rock and down the basalt ridge to the high point of the Tundel farm. He dismounted and slumped against a rock. Still carried away by adrenaline, Virgil threw his hands over his face and began laughing out loud.

Chapter 5

FEARING MORE MISCHIEF, and at the sheriff's insistence, both Lacrosse and Boone Crowe slept at the jail, stretching out on lumpy bunks in separate cells. But the marshal had risen early, saddled Hunter and set out for the small hamlet on the outskirts of town where it was rumored the one-armed preacher held shop. He plodded in the gray-red dawn past the office of Dr. T. T. Wills and wondered at the fate of Ike Werth. If he found the preacher, and if he learned anything of value, he might stop back by the Doc's and see if the deadly old Rebel had survived Hunter's blow.

A quarter of a mile east of Fort Tillman a shanty of approximately fifteen tents of various sizes and condition nestled sleepily against a hillside. He followed the beaten horse path into its midst, noticing the eyes of three or four early-risers sizing him up. They appeared nearly identical, standing in dirty shirts, their suspenders hanging limp at their hips, faces grizzled with unkempt whiskers, hair long and tangled. Both had tarnished hoglegs jammed into their waistbands and they stared at Crowe in stupid defiance. Beyond these men he saw a woman just then emerge from a tent, standing in her bloomers with a blanket wrapped around her shoulders. Dark, worn out makeup marked her eyes and half-rubbed off lipstick smeared her lips.

Crowe pulled Hunter to a stop in front of this woman and nodded. "You familiar with the one-armed preacher?" he asked.

The woman let out a sudden cackle that shook her piled-up hair. "Not as familiar as I'd like to be. Ha! But I'm workin on him."

The marshal couldn't resist a smile of his own. "So, he's here."

"Yup. He and Deacon John occupy that little chapel right over there." She laughed again, and pointed a finger in the direction of a ragamuffin tent further up the path.

Crowe glanced at the indicated tent then back at her. "Who is Deacon John?"

"He's the blood that follows wherever the preacher goes. He's a handsome one, that one. Tall for an Injun. But his voice…his voice is like a quail's voice. Sweet." She batted her blackened eyelashes dramatically and then laughed once more.

The marshal nudged Hunter away from this woman and her mischief and stopped before the so-called chapel, another of the woman's jests. He dismounted and moved toward the entrance then stopped. From inside he could hear murmurings. He bent his head closer to the tent flap and listened.

"…and the prayer offered in faith will heal the sick, and the Lord will raise him up, and if he has committed sins, they will be forgiven him. Amen."

A second voice, deeper, repeated, "Amen."

Crowe retreated a few steps from the tent and after a moment cleared his throat with great expression. Then he saw the stub of a half-arm protrude and cast the tent flap aside, followed by the man himself, a medium-sized fellow with suntanned face and graying temples. His eyes were bright and his cheeks shaven clean, but with a duly impressive mustache angling down to his chin. There was something dazzling about his appearance, something altogether unearthly.

"Welcome, brother," he said in greeting.

The marshal gave a faltered nod.

"Have you come to worship? Services begin in an hour. I try to get to their souls early, before the whisky does." He said this without jest.

Crowe looked down at the preacher's missing arm, which disappeared a few inches below his right elbow and which was uncovered and tanned like the rest of him. Even though the marshal was over six-foot, he had the strange sensation that this little man was somehow taller than him. "Worship?" he answered clumsily. He shook his head. "No. I...I came to ask you a question."

"Splendid," the preacher said and pointed through the tent flap to a crude wooden table encircled by equally crude benches. "When John and I are not eating or sleeping, this, through the mystery of God, becomes the sanctuary of the church. Please enter."

Crowe looked around him, saw that the woman was gone but that the two men at the other end of the shanty were still watching him. He sighed, took off his hat and ducked inside the tent. The morning sun threw golden beams in through holes and tears in the canvas, giving the interior an odd, saintly appearance. And bent over a small, soot-charred wood stove stood a youngish dignified fellow in a dusty black suit and neatly combed black hair. Before him were the makings of a pot of coffee.

"John, say hello to our guest, whose name I have not yet received."

The marshal felt suddenly large inside these confines, what with his heavy coat and his many pistols. He fumbled with his hat and said, "Crowe. Marshal Boone Crowe."

"Marshal Crowe indeed. A pleasure to meet a fellow man of peace."

"What—"

The preacher chuckled. "Aren't you what they call a 'peace officer'?"

Crowe looked at the Indian named John then back to the preacher.

"You and I," the preacher said. "We clearly use different methods, but in the end, well…without sounding unkind, you weed out the more difficult cases while I am left with those who remain. Those more fortunate ones who may actually give thought to their sins and repent." All this was said with that peculiar winsome smile.

Finally, the Indian turned from the stove and extended a tin cup of steaming coffee. "Sit down, Marshal. But watch that. It's hot."

Crowe took the cup and sat down across from the preacher. Deacon John sat on a stool nearby and stirred some sugar into his own cup. "Sugar, Marshal?"

"No thanks."

They all sat in dumb silence for a long moment, the marshal gazing at the greasy stains in the tent canvas, then at the two cots and two footlockers. On the table next to the preacher laid a Bible and his eyes focused on this for another prolonged moment. Finally he spoke. "I'm looking for someone."

The preacher nodded understandingly. "Most of us are," he said.

Crowe pulled out his watch and toyed with it for a second, then opened it and held it up to the preacher. The one-armed man leaned close and gazed at the dim photograph inside the watch cap. From Crowe's vest pocket, he removed a pair of spectacles and attaching them to his nose and around his ears, he narrowed his gaze onto the black and white figure printed there, studying it intimately. He motioned for John to look also and after some concentration the Indian nodded.

"You've seen her then," Crowe said, looking from one man and then to the other.

"I always meet the train, Marshal. That is, when I'm not out riding the circuit. I like to keep track of the new arrivals. For my own reasons, you understand."

Deacon John nodded his handsome head. His eyes gleamed like onyx stones. "If that is the same lady—two months ago. Train from Omaha. I remember because it was the same train Walking Fox Carter came on."

"Who is Walking Fox Carter?" Crowe asked.

"He is an old half-breed trapper. Old as the grass."

"But the woman. You think it was her."

Both clergymen nodded.

"Did you talk to her? Did she say where she was going?

How long ago did you say? Two months?"

The preacher was still examining the tintype. "Is she your wife, Marshal? Your sister?"

The lawman took back the watch and returned it to his vest pocket. "Neither."

"A friend then. You need not be timid, Marshal. I hear the gravest of stories related to me in some very dark hours. In dark hours of the soul, you understand. My own heart carries the confessions of hundreds."

His words came with difficulty. "Her name is Eva Gist. She was coming from Omaha. We have known each other a long time. She sent me a telegram that she would be stopping here, at Fort Tillman. She wanted to visit a friend for a couple of days. Then she would be back on the train. And coming on to Buffalo to…to meet me." His eyes seemed to lose their focus. "She did not arrive."

"I'm sorry, Marshal Crowe. We don't know much more. She'd been wearing a bonnet against the sun but just as she detrained, she pulled it back. Otherwise I may not have recognized her by your photograph. She seemed to acknowledge that I was a man of the cloth by my attire. Or so I assumed. And she gave me a pleasant hello. I tipped my hat. And beyond that, I know nothing else."

"Was there anyone meeting her? Another woman?"

"Not at first," interjected Deacon John. "I lingered, talking with old man Carter. Your lady friend stood beside her bag for maybe ten minutes. Finally a buckboard arrived and she climbed in and they left town immediately."

"Tell me—who was driving the buckboard?"

"I may be a civilized Redman, Marshal Crowe, but I am still a Redman. And smart Indians, even Christianized Indians, have learned to mind their own business."

"But if you saw her get in a wagon then you must have seen who was driving it."

"A man and a young girl. That's all I remember. I had my back to them mostly. Walking Fox Carter was facing them. And he's long gone now."

"Long gone?"

"Back into the mountains."

"The young girl then. How old a girl?"

Deacon John rose up off the stool and walked to the tent flap, tossed it aside and left. Crowe started to go after him but the one-armed preacher placed a hand on the marshal's shoulder, indicating him to wait. "He's just thinking. He needs to think. He'll be back."

Boone Crowe looked at his coffee cup with disinterest but took a drink in spite of it. He sighed deeply.

"Perhaps she became ill," the preacher said. "Or more likely, someone in the family she is visiting became ill and is helping care for them."

"But why no message?"

"That I cannot answer. I like to believe we live in enlightened times, Marshal. But the two corpses still being showcased on Main Street proves me mistaken."

"News travels fast."

"Not necessarily, Marshal. But I make my rounds."

After several torturous minutes the Indian returned. He stood in the doorway with the gray sky at his back and his hands folded before him. "The girl appeared older than ten but not yet fifteen. The man used a cane."

The marshal looked at the young man, his black suit and black string tie dusty but not dirty. Standing, Crowe nodded at the preacher, who remained seated, and then turning shook the Indian's hand. "If you learn more, tell Sheriff Hoody. He'll know how to get in touch with me."

"Godspeed," the young man said, his onyx, unblemished eyes shining.

When the two remaining riders on the Melgoza range rode out to relieve their partners they were greeted with a confusing scene. The herd had bolted and ran a mile farther up the draw toward the line shack. The two riders, Jones and Tally, followed the draw back down to where their partners should have been and found what looked like a massacre—a dozen dead animals and two dead cowboys. Every clue pointed to a bushwhacking so Jones and Tally quickly drew straws to see who would stay with the herd and who would ride like hell back to Starkweather and give him the news. Neither man had any desire to do either task, but Jones drew the straw to stay with the herd, so Tally left immediately. But before he had gone two hundred yards he picked up the trail of the assassin—shell casings in the dirt proved it—and decided to follow that instead.

Brady Quinn had ridden through the night, cutting every wire he came to. At one point, in the middle of the night, he thought he heard the faint, roaring echo of a rifle shot, but it was too far away to be certain. Fumbling in the dark he made slow work of his job. He knew the route the herd would probably take, so he made sure that the wires were not only cut, but also drug off to the side so as not to tangle the stampede when it came. It was nearing dawn and he was wearily ambling through the ravine that divided the Ashmun range from the Tundel farm when he came upon an unexpected scene. Sitting on a rock with his face in his hands, his horse tied off at a clump of sage, sat Virgil Tundel.

And Tundel was laughing.

Too involved in his merriment, Virgil did not hear Brady Quinn approach. Dismounting cautiously, Quinn sidled behind a thorny tree and watched while the farmer attempted to regain control of his amusement. Virgil rose from his rock and walked to his horse, lifting a canteen from his saddle horn and took a deep drink. He had barely finished, drawing it back from his mouth when he saw Quinn's horse, and then the killer himself, standing but thirty yards away.

"Mornin Virgil. Good day for a laugh, huh."

"You sonofabitch."

"Don't be sad, old pard. You're goin to be joinin your brother soon now."

Virgil stood behind his horse, shielding himself, trying to remember where he'd laid his Sharps. He spied it then, propped against the rock where he'd been sitting.

Quinn saw it too. "Shame how things work out, ain't it?"

Virgil felt his blood pitch in his veins. Never one to carry a sidearm, he cursed himself now. Then slowly, staying on the far side of his horse, he began leading it toward the rock and to his Sharps.

"That won't do, Virgil. You'll never make it."

Virgil kept moving though, faster now, so Quinn pulled a pistol and put a shot between the horse's legs. The bullet tore at the rocks, throwing splinters of shale in the air. The horse bolted then and Virgil, holding on, tried still to steer it toward his Sharps. Quinn's next shot went through Virgil's wrist and now his horse pulled away completely and left him standing in the open, twenty feet from his rifle.

"You Tundel's jist don't get it, do you. Do we have to kill all you men-folk before you finally pack up?"

They stood facing each other in the dawn, silent, almost casually, as if both men were waiting for a train.

The pain in his left wrist was starting to register and Virgil could feel the blood oozing over his hand and onto the ground. He staggered for a second, amazed at how much blood there was. His heart seemed like a pump, like the hand pump at the well in the yard, the swish and surge of his heart. He could hear it, beating, pumping.

"You're bleedin pretty heavy, Virgil. You might want to sit down."

His head was beginning to hurt. How could a simple shot through the wrist cause him to feel this way? So soon. And yet the blood seemed to pulse out of him like a running brook.

Brady Quinn remained at a distance. He had intended to talk some more. Then kill him quickly. But he was mesmerized by what was happening before his very eyes. A shot through the wrist—a lucky shot—had severed a main vein, he supposed, and now the oldest Tundel son was literally having the lifeblood drain out of him, like a turned over bottle of whisky without a cork.

For Virgil's part, his profound hatred of Quinn—for all he had done and all he represented—blinded him to the reality that he was bleeding to death. Not once, standing there, did he consider stopping the spigot-like flow of blood. Instead they stood apart like a pair of duelists; like a bull and a matador. He turned and looked at his Sharps again but it seemed far away now. Finally his knees buckled and he found himself lying on the sandstone.

"You've made my work too easy, Tundel. I thought we might chat a while longer. But you done went and left the party."

Virgil felt himself swooning. He thought about his night. About the cattle he'd shot. And the riders. And it started to blend into darkness. He thought he heard Junson's voice, close in his ear. At last he thought about the corn. And the pumpkins. But not once did he think about Lucy.

August Tundel, ambling toward the barn with the milk bucket saw that one of the horses was missing, and stood in momentary puzzlement. He turned finally and strode to Virgil and Lucy's portion of the house to tell his brother that someone might have stolen some livestock. But before he could reach the door, it swung open and standing in the shadowed doorframe was Lucy, still in yesterday's clothes, her hair undone. Meeting August's gaze she spoke with scorn, "He's not here."

He studied her face; saw the sleepless weariness there. "Where'd he go?"

She turned her hands over, showing her palms. "He didn't say. Not exactly. But you know who he's after."

August nodded. He kept his eyes on her. "Even after Pa told him not to."

"Virgil ain't one to be told," she said. Then realizing she looked poorly, she put her hands up to her face, and then to her hair. "You better tell your father."

It was half an hour before Lucy appeared again, her face scrubbed to pinkness and her hair in a braid. The rest of the family was sitting around the table in the kitchen, an assortment of soiled dishes scattered about.

"We held some biscuits for you, honey," Ma said. "And some applesauce. We waited on you like the pigs we are." These were the first casual words August's mother had spoken since they'd buried Junson. Normally everybody would have been about his or her daily chores, but a stew of anger, grief and disorder had sidelined all normal routine. Now, with Virgil still not back from wherever it was he had gone, nerves were bare once again.

Lucy sat on the bench next to August where a clean plate

was set for her, but she made no effort to eat. She looked into the face of each person present, and then told them all that she knew, about Virgil wanting revenge, and that Pa's way of sitting around and doing nothing was the wrong way. That somebody in this family needed to take action. He said that that somebody would be him. Ma Tundel gave a low, sorrowful groan, but Pa only sat there thumbing the mug that held his cooling coffee.

It was an hour later, while Pa was on the top end of the cornfield steering water down through the cornrows, and August was greasing some harnesses in the barn, that the pounding echo of thunder roiled up over the upper hillock. It was all Pa could do but turn, shovel in hand, before the first of Starkweather's cattle lifted off the hill like a tidal wave and bore down onto the Tundel homestead.

August dashed from the barn in time to see Pa standing before the frenzied herd, struggling to pull a pistol from his waistband before being overtaken by the noise and the dust. As August ran toward the house he could now see riders flanking the herd and by the time he reached the door, Lucy had already retrieved the coyote rifle from its pegs and was shoving it into August's hands. Ma was holding a shotgun but Lucy took it from her. All three of them stood in horror as the mob of frantic livestock made a crazy swath directly through the pasture and then down onto the crop fields, sidestepping the barn and corrals but swinging wide and tearing up the vegetable garden as they galloped directly in front of the house. They heard gunshots now too, coming from the riders.

For a moment it was too much to take in. August stood frozen. Then a steer veered off and lowering its head came straight for him. Shaken out of his shock, August fired the rifle from his hip and the steer fell to its knees and then over. Now, through the tumult, he began shooting toward the dust-shrouded riders.

"Get down!

It was Lucy's voice behind him. He could feel her hand on his shoulder and felt her breath at his ear. "Get down."

They both dropped to their knees, August finally realizing that he was a duck in a pond, standing there in the middle of the yard. Bullets were hitting the side of the house now, making dull thuds, and they both looked back to see if Ma was still standing in the doorway, but she was not. Turning, August fired again. The trailing end of the cattle was coming into view, a lone rider driving them. August blinked through the grit in his eyes and took aim. His rifle bucked and the rider, throwing his arms wide, slumped in the saddle, the horse riding on.

In another half-minute the thing was over, the last of the stampede winding through a wide gully and up over the next hill. They knelt there in stunned silence, as the blur of dust seemed to follow the cattle, the last of its grit throwing an eerie red glow over the morning sun. The devastation was supreme. In three short minutes the ground had been turned over and the crops flattened. Even the handful of pigs and sheep had been trampled, fences torn down, and the corn beaten into unrecognizable fodder. And Pa. Where was Pa?

The whole landscape seemed foreign now and August had a hard time fixing himself in the right direction of the cornfield and where he'd last seen Pa. Leaving Lucy, he ran across the battered yard and up the hill, but before he reached the top he saw his father rise up out of the head ditch, wet and caked with mud, but standing. When they came together they stared at each other wordlessly, the old man's pistol still in his hand.

Finally, old man Tundel spoke. "The women. They okay?"

August looked back over his shoulder and saw Lucy and his mother standing with slumped shoulders, Ma knocking dust from Lucy's apron.

The two men did not survey the damage as the dreadfulness of it spoke for itself. Instead they plodded through the upturned earth looking for other things. Near where the pigs had once gathered in their flimsy board corral and where they now laid bloody and trampled they found a rider, half trampled himself and dead. And further, where August had placed his concentrated shot, laid a second rider, blood pumping from a bullet hole in his stomach. His eyes batted in confounded distress.

The elder Tundel glared down at him then looked off at the surrounding hills to make sure no one was coming back. "This is Starkweather's doings, ain't it?"

The crippled rider's eyes widened. "Please...help me. I'm gut shot."

"Starkweather called for this, didn't he," Tundel asked again.

The rider, fighting tears, affirmed this with a painful nod of his head.

August was amazed at his father's calm voice. It did not exhibit the malice he knew both of them were feeling inside.

"See what that fiend brought down on you, son. Sent you on a fool's errand. Now look at you. All shot to hell and dying. Tell me. Was it worth it?"

It was hard for August to look at this rider, a kid as young as himself. He looked at his pa and the old man tilted his head toward the house. "Go look after the women. Yer mother's probably needin to see yer face."

The rider knew. And August knew. He turned and trudged to the house. Lucy was standing by the well, her face set like stone, her eyes were the only alive thing in her expression. Then came the sharp report of Pa's pistol.

After leaving the preacher's tent, Marshal Boone Crowe rode directly atop a surrounding bluff that overlooked the town of Fort Tillman and sat his saddle in silence. He was feeling his age this morning. He was feeling lost. The interview he had hoped would shed light on Eva's whereabouts amounted to nothing. Or next to nothing. She had disembarked the train; Deacon John had witnessed that much. And he saw her get into a buckboard; rather this Walking Fox Carter saw her.

Crowe dismounted Hunter and let the reins drop. Looking eastward he gazed somberly at the line of railroad tracks that snaked through the hills approaching Fort Tillman.

"She was on that train," he muttered to himself. She had been coming to see him, just as they had planned. Once in Buffalo, they would ride together out to the little ranch he planned to buy. It was still for sale and Tub Murray was this very day waiting for his final word on it. *I'll hold it for you, Boone. You figure out the details. Let me know. She's a beaut.* But here he was now, searching for the better half of the bargain—Eva Gist. He knew her from childhood. Their fathers were neighboring farmers. While Boone was gone fighting for the Union, she had married a man from Nebraska and moved away. He saw her ten years later outside of Omaha while he was a deputy marshal. She was a widow by then, so he showed her the more gentle side of himself, the part that was not lawman or soldier. She was too good for him, he knew. But last year, while transporting a prisoner to Omaha, he stopped to see her, her face ever present in his thoughts. *Come out to Wyoming and take a look. I've got my eye on a spread. If you like it, and if you can settle on an old man like me, well... we could be married.* She smiled at him, tugging playfully at the frills of his vest. *I'm listening,* she said.

He returned to Hunter and swung almost violently into the saddle. He stared westward this time, back to Dry Branch and to the Tundel's and all the mess that surrounded them. He wanted no part of it. There seemed to be no marshaling in him anymore. Let the younger men fight these wars. It was time—well past time—to hang up the badge and simply disappear. He had killed in the war and he had killed men in the streets. He had even killed a man just a day ago. There would be no end to the killing.

Back down the bluff he rode, toward Fort Tillman, to resume the bitter search for the woman he could now admit, he had always loved.

Ethan Moss, Starkweather's foreman, did not take part in the stampede through Tundel's land, he simply told the riders what the boss wanted done. Then he rode ahead to report to Starkweather himself about the killings of cattle and men up on the Melgoza Range.

Half way to the ranch he crossed trails with Tally who had followed the assassin's trail to Ashmun's corral, and was riding hell-bent to report to Starkweather.

"Whoa," Moss roared, cutting Tally off in his gallop. "You got Injuns after you."

Tally pulled up fiercely, swung out of his saddle, and threw himself on the ground. "Damn, Ethan. Did you hear what happened up on the range?"

"I just came from there."

"Well, I know who did it," Tally panted.

"Who?"

"I followed his trail. It was like followin the smell a' bread to the kitchen. It was Ashmun. Or one of his men."

"Ashmun," Moss bellowed. "Are you sure?"

Tally told his foreman the whole story of finding the

worn out, still-saddled horse, and all the signs of the trail that led to it.

"Saddle up, pard," Moss said. "We best make our report."

The two men rode slower now, Moss trying to make sense of what he'd just learned. Was Ashmun making a move against Starkweather now? He was pretty sure both ranchers were vying for the same prize—to run the whole range, free of competition. It would be a cattle kingdom for the winner, and it reminded him of two great thunderbolts striking each other. Napoleon and Cromwell. With poor Tundel and his brood, caught in the middle. Well, probably not for much longer, he thought. If the boys did their job this morning, Tundel will be all but finished, and he wasn't exactly sure how he felt about that.

When the two riders reached the ranch and relayed the information they had gathered, they saw their boss fly into a menacing rage. Starkweather jerked Tally from his horse and knocked him to the ground with his fist. Then he kicked him.

"Where were you when those cattle were being killed?" he yelled.

Tally, covering up, tried to stop him with his words. "It...it weren't my...watch, boss. Jones and...and me wasn't due till this morning. That's when we found the dead cattle. And...and Cy and Tommy. Dead. Don't hit me...boss."

But Starkweather did hit him, again and again, until Ethan Moss dismounted and intervened. "Boss. There's more. Stop and listen." He stepped back then, fearfully, and waited while his words sank in, shooting a hateful glance at Jack Stone, who had been watching the entire incident with satisfaction, leaning against a rail, a pleased smile across his dark face.

Starkweather straightened up, pulling at the front of his vest and picking up his hat, which he had lost in the fray. He turned to Moss, his face still crimson with rage. His hand moved down to his pistol and Moss feared, for a moment, that his boss might actually draw on him. Slowly Starkweather's breathing steadied and he met Moss's eye.

"Tally here followed the assassin's trail," Moss said. He looked down at the rider, who was bleeding from the nose, his left eye swelling, and watched him struggle to his knees. "Tell him what you found."

Tally looked close to tears, so shocked by his unfair beating. Eyes downcast, he told his boss everything he knew.

Jack Stone's smile widened. "Ashmun," he said, curiously.

At that very moment, coming down through the draw behind the corrals, rode Brady Quinn. He was astride his horse, and was leading another horse by its reins, a dead man stretched over the saddle.

Tally gathered himself to his feet, standing well away from Starkweather as he, Moss, and Stone watched Quinn trot into the yard. "Merry Christmas, Mr. Starkweather. I brought you a present."

Starkweather stepped up to the horse and lifted the dead man's head by his hair. "Well, I'll be damned. Virgil Tundel.

Cold as a mackerel."

Ethan Moss stepped away from the group, feeling sick. Brady's words sounded hollow to his ears as the young killer retold the tale of bleeding Virgil Tundel out with a shot to the wrist.

"It was like watching a pig die. 'Cept he never once squealed. I gotta hand it to him, boss. He died good. Never complained. Just stood there, stupid as an Indian."

Starkweather forgot all about Tally, and for the moment, Ashmun. He patted Quinn vigorously on the shoulder. "Now listen. Here's what I want you to do. Get yourself a fresh horse. Then ride into Dry Branch. And take Tundel with you. I want him put in a pine box and leaned up against the Bright's store. And I want a sign put on him. Understand? I want a sign in big letters. 'Death to squatters'. What'd you think boys?" He turned to Jack Stone. "What'd you think," he said again.

"I'm not big for advertising," Stone said, spitting a glob of worn out tobacco into the dirt. "I think just the body in the box will be good enough. Let those corn-eaters come to their own conclusions. And one that Ashmun will understand too."

Starkweather did not like to be contradicted, but this business with Ashmun now would need some thinking. "Fine. Just the body in a box." He turned to Quinn. "See that it gets done."

Off to the side, Moss handed Tally his neckerchief and told him to clean himself up. Both men had been in the saddle long hours and needed rest, and each hoped that the ugliness of this day would not find them drawn in deeper. The cattle would be coming in soon and that would bring to their ears a tale of further misery for the Tundels.

To the west an ominous sky was turning black. Hours earlier Tee Blake had turned his horse in that direction hoping to run into Ward Ashmun himself. He had gotten nowhere with his daughter and wasn't in the bargain for a long wait. If those clouds held snow, then Ashmun would be looking to move his cattle down quick, and an extra hand might be his ticket.

It was nearing noon when he spied the chuck wagon on the next rise, and a ring of cowboys huddled against the approaching wind. In their center stood old man Ashmun, his long graying hair blowing under his pulled down hat. Every now and then Blake saw him pointing, as if giving directions, so his gradual approach was mostly unnoticed. When he finally did reach the circle of riders, the old man stopped talking and turned to see who had come up on them. Paying Blake no mind, he looked back at his men and said, "Now get to it," and they all swung their horses around and rode off to perform their various duties.

"What do you want?" Ashmun asked gruffly, not looking at the young man. He strode toward the chuck wagon.

The cowboy nudged his horse and followed slowly. "Names Tee Blake, sir."

"I know who you are. Did Starkweather send you to give me a message?"

"No sir. I ain't with him no more."

Reaching the wagon, Ashmun finally turned, studying the cowboy. "He run you off?"

"No sir. Nothing of the kind. I run myself off. I'm a cowman, Mr. Ashmun. Not a gunslinger. The job was gettin too complicated for me."

Ashmun let Blake's words sink in. "Get down then. Get some coffee in you."

Tee Blake obeyed, tying his horse's reins to the wagon wheel. Ashmun handed him a cup of the black, steaming coffee, and continued sizing up his guest.

"I'm currently jobless, sir. I'll starve before I'll do any more of what Starkweather was askin."

"What was he asking?"

Blake fidgeted uncomfortably. Mr. Ashmun knew how to get to the heart of matters and it unsettled him. "Well…I guess he's trying real hard to tie up the land. He's got his eyes set on running Ernest Tundel off."

"That's no secret, son." The old man took a drink from his cup. "I don't pay much attention to other people's business. But I wouldn't be surprised if Starkweather was behind those burnings. The Hamm brothers. And those other folks."

Tee dropped his head. "The Woodsons."

"So it's true."

Blake nodded solemnly. "But…but I was not part of that. He…Starkweather… he's got men he calls on to do that. I was not asked to go. And wouldn't have if asked."

"Then why'd you quit him?"

"Mr. Ashmun. I come up here hopin to get a job."

"I asked you why you quit him."

Blake looked into his coffee cup but did not drink. He thought for a moment that he might just get back in the saddle and ride away. But there was power in the old man's voice, a commanding power that seemed to demand an answer. "Fear, I reckon. I saw the marshal kill one of our riders a couple of days ago. Shot him right out of his saddle. And I was not five feet away. It could have been me. Then…" His hand went instinctively to his scalp where the Sharps bullet had grazed him. "I was ordered to watch the Tundel place night before last. I didn't want to do it. Someone—I reckon one of the Tundels—took a shot at me in the dark. I was lucky again. I got no fight with the Tundels. Got no fight with anybody."

Both men were silent for a while. Ashmun turned his collar up against the wind. "What'd you make of them clouds, Blake?"

The cowboy looked up. "Snow, I would guess."

"That's my thought too."

Again, more silence. "You said a marshal killed your partner? What marshal would that be?"

"Starkweather knew him. Called him Crowe."

"Marshal Boone Crowe." Ashmun showed surprise. "Two days ago, you say?"

"Yessir. About then."

"What was Crowe doing down here, messing around

with Starkweather?"

"One of Starkweather's men, kid name of Quinn, gunned down the Tundel boy in Dry Branch."

Ashmun nodded. "Heard about that. My daughter Freya was all worked up over it. Rode out here fretting in a big way." He put his cup down on the wagon board and rubbed his palms together. "I suppose I wasn't very kind to her. Caught me at a bad time. But..." He looked squarely into Blake's eyes. "You understand, I have no great sympathy for the squatters myself." He mused upon his own remarks for a spell, and then added, "Still, I am no Starkweather. I don't abide by murder."

"Then you understand my quittin."

"Put that way, I guess I do."

The first white flakes of snow began to fall two hills to the west, slanting with the wind and laying hazy wallpaper before the distant mountains. Both men watched knowingly, but neither moved.

"She's a filly I can't seem to break. Freya, that is. And here I've stood, giving you more time than I gave her yesterday. On the list of fatherly crimes, I reckon that's a big one."

Tee Blake made no comment. The black, snow-filled clouds moved quickly, rubbing their bellies against the high hills and dumping their leafy whiteness as they roiled nearer. Blake saw that the old man was a long ways off in his thoughts and the young cowboy felt increasingly uncomfortable. "About that job, sir."

Ward Ashmun came out of his reverie slowly, looking

around as if waking up. He looked at Blake. "How are you on a horse?"

"None better, sir. Even when I got shot, I stayed astride." His hand again strayed up to his scalp, touching the tender crease.

"See that fellow over yonder?" He pointed. "That's Wes Bridges. He's my foreman. You ride up there and tell him you're on the payroll."

Blake beamed. "Thank you, sir." He climbed into the saddle, still holding the cup, then realizing it, he got back down and put the cup onto the wagon board, then leapt into the saddle again. He took off his wide-brimmed hat and tipped it in a salute to Ashmun, then beat it against his horse's flanks lovingly and spurred the critter to a gallop.

Old man Ashmun watched the kid ride away, and then turned his face to the approaching snow, and the bleak signs of an early Wyoming winter.

Young Tanner Hornfisher sat on the front porch of the little shack whittling on a block of wood. Beside him, sitting in his sightless, voiceless void, was the old Indian called Coyote. The boy turned the block from side to side, slicing off leafs of soft, white wood.

Occasionally Tanner would tap Coyote on the knee and hand the wood to him for his inspection. The Indian would let his brown fingers do his seeing for him, stroking each notch with serious interest, then passed it back to the boy.

A cold wind was sending tumbleweeds and debris down through the main street of Dry Branch as the black clouds in the west drew nearer. Across the street rang the rhythmic blows of Hornfisher's heavy hammer striking his anvil. Occasionally the whoosh of his billows joined-in and the scattering of sparks flew from the blacksmith's fire. Faintly then, came the first sounds of horses' hoof beats, coming slowly from the east, and Tanner told Coyote he would be right back, he wanted to see who was coming into town.

Rounding the corner of the livery stable doors, young Tanner Hornfisher suddenly felt his heart jump. He tried immediately to swallow but could not muster the spit needed. A rush of anger and fear turned his face hot as he saw, to his instant dread, the killer Brady Quinn plodding toward him into town. And behind him came a second horse, one that carried the body of another man, either dead or wounded, slumped across the saddle. Tanner felt his hair tingle with hatred. Keen to the sounds around him, he suddenly grew aware that his father's hammer had ceased banging. When he looked up he saw him standing beside the billows, stained leather apron showing dull in the shadows, his stern expression revealing a shared distress.

Brady Quinn passed between them in parade attitude. At the front of Amos' store he pulled up, but before he could holler out, Amos Bright emerged from within.

"You got an undertaker in this town," Quinn said, louder than necessary, and with an edge of satisfied mirth in his voice.

Amos looked at the body across the horse. "We never

needed one till you came along."

Ignoring this, Quinn went on. "This here fellow met with a sad end up on the range. He needs a burying. Mr. Starkweather thought you might oughta put him on display until he could be…claimed."

"Leave him," Amos said. "We'll take care of it. Just leave."

Quinn pulled his sombrero down against the wind. "You know, it's a mighty dry ride comin down here. A drink would suit me fine."

A voice came from behind him. "Do your drinking somewhere else." It was Matthew Hornfisher, and he was standing in the street, his double-barrel shotgun braced across his arms. His face shown flinty, his eyes black as pellets.

Quinn turned his horse and faced him. "You must be crazy."

Behind the batwing doors of the saloon, Clive Leyland emerged from the shadows, watching. Across the street, Little George stepped from an alleyway and stood, white-faced and skittish. He recognized Virgil's horse, and then recognized Virgil too, and a sick misery swept over him. And Tanner Hornfisher, alarmed at seeing his father taking such a dangerous stand, walked solemnly into the street and crept up to his side.

"Get back, Tanner," Hornfisher ordered, but the boy did not move.

"I see you got your protector there, Mr. Blacksmith. Nerves of steel, huh."

Hornfisher shifted his shotgun, adding to its menace. He felt Tanner move against his leg and he stiffened.

"You better tell that boy of yours to get back," Quinn said in a whisper. Then he looked down at Tanner. "Yer pa is a mighty brave man, sonny. But he ain't very smart." His right hand let go of the reins and began the slow descent toward the butt of his pistol, but stopped when he heard Hornfisher click back both hammers on the shotgun.

Suddenly Tanner's voice shot out, unexpected as a snakebite. "I hate you," he shouted. "I *hate* you." It was almost a scream, and there was venom in his words.

Quinn threw his head back in shock, poisoned by the boy's shocking bitterness. He sat his saddle for a moment as if in a daze, as if he could not believe the words. Finally he looked back to Hornfisher with weak resolve. "Mr. Starkweather," he started then paused. "He…he will not be happy to hear this. Any of this." Then, with a spur dug into his horse's flanks, he threw off the reins to the lead horse and made a showy dash down the street and out into the range.

The town released its collective breath. Finally Amos looked at Hornfisher and said, "You're a damn fool, Matthew. He would have killed you with a laugh."

Hornfisher said nothing, but in a moment LG was there to share the terrible knowledge—the dead man is Virgil Tundel.

Snow reached Fort Tillman by late afternoon. Boone Crowe

watched it fall from Dr. Wills' office window. Lying on a slab of mattress in a dim corner was Ike Werth, a dent the size of a teacup, with the imprint of a horseshoe, fixed against his skull. Both eyes were black and his nose, stuffed with cotton, showed the red of seeping blood. The doctor, seated across from Crowe, was pouring each of them a glass of whisky.

"I expected him to give it up last night," Wills said. "I've seen a fair amount of this sort of thing. Most die within hours. The shock alone, not to mention damage to the brain."

"Ike Werth never started with many brains," Crowe said through his whisky. "Being stupid must be a deterrent to death. At least in his case."

Dr. Wills smiled but made no comment.

The marshal asked the doctor if there was anything he might know about the woman, Eva Gist, who he was looking for. He spoke freely now, realizing that his former shyness about her, and the subject of love in general, would only hamper his pursuit of answers. But the doctor knew nothing. In fact, he had been out of town, fulfilling some doctoral duties, the day she supposedly arrived on the train.

Before Boone Crowe left the doctor's office, he asked once more about Ike Werth's prospects.

"If he regains consciousness, it will be a miracle. But if he does, it will tell the tale. He may end up being simple as a turnip. It's hard to say."

Back on the street, Marshal Crowe stood beneath a poled awning and watched the snow in its flurrying tempest. The storm matched his mood. There was nothing here, he realized. Nothing more to know. Whisky always tightened his nerves. He shouldn't touch the stuff, he thought, staring at the snow.

In his bank of memories, he saw once again the Tennessee countryside. As a major he was leading his men on a morning foraging party when they got caught in a freak snowstorm. He and his men sat their horses, concealed in a thicket, watching the spectacle. It had been one of the most unusually peaceful moments he had experienced in the war, and he remembered not wanting to move from that place. Later, there had been rifle fire in the distance and when they maneuvered their way along a trampled down cornfield, they saw the field littered with newly killed soldiers, Reb and Yank alike, the snow turned red with the blood of dead men.

He gazed up at the snow again from where it came swirling out of the sky and thought about Eva Gist. He suspected the worst now. But what was the worst? Had she changed her mind about meeting him and gone back to Omaha? He secretly wouldn't have blamed her. But in his heart now, he feared even worse things. It was time he accepted the possibility that—

"You look like a man about to commit a crime."

It was Rud Lacrosse, coming up the boardwalk beside him.

"Only in my mind," he answered, wryly.

"You ate yet?"

"No. I just drank my breakfast with the doc."

"Oh, Doc Wills. How's his patient?"

"He's alive. Just barely. Hunter caved him in pretty good."

"You fixin to leave? You look like it."

"I am," Crowe said.

"Didn't find who you were looking for?"

Crowe shook his head. "Just dead ends."

"What's next for you then? A long ride back to Buffalo?"

"I reckon."

"No more business with Starkweather then?"

"Maybe. Nothing to concern you though. Not unless you want to get hung again."

"I wasn't planning on it. But when you get around to hanging Starkweather, I'd appreciate an invitation."

"You'd like to see that, huh?"

"I'd like to be the one puts the noose around his neck."

"You might have to win that right away from old man Tundel."

"He the feller that had his son killed?"

Crowe nodded gravely. "I'm heading there today. I told him I'd stop back by. You interested in riding along?"

Lacrosse shook his head. "I don't think you'd approve of my kind of justice."

Boone Crowe eyed the younger man with considerable scrutiny. "You might know, Rud, I had a good reason for staying out of this fight. I was planning on retiring. Eva Gist and I were going to be wed. As long as she'd have me, that is. I already put some money down on a little spread east of Buffalo, just to hold it. It was going to be the end of my marshaling days. No more fighting. No more killing." He paused for a breath. He wasn't used to talking this much. But confessions were rare and it might be his last one.

"Nothing wrong with plans like that."

"Except Eva's nowhere to be found. And that has not put me in the best of moods. So if I happen to run into Starkweather again, I might just kill him out of spite. He's an old enemy and he should have been dead a long time ago."

They moved together down the boardwalk and stopped in front of The Derby House but did not go in. The aroma of bacon and coffee was strong but neither man made a move to go inside.

"Judge Schaffer probably thinks I'm a coward," Lacrosse said.

"He probably thinks you're dead. It was a fool's errand to begin with, sending one man to do the job of a posse."

"I had that very same thought. When I was swinging off the ground."

"I can see how that might be."

"Well, I am no coward. But I had a lot of time to think since then. Strange thing. I got over feeling sorry for myself the first week or so. It's those other folks I keep thinking about. The families Starkweather burned out. Maybe I been listening to too many of that one-armed preacher's sermons. But I'd swear I was growing a conscience."

Boone Crowe shook his head. "Hard to do any serious killing when you've got a conscience like that?"

"You've hit on the very problem, Boone. My conscience don't cover men like Starkweather. Or anybody who rides with him. There must be some awful sin in that kind of thinking."

"You might be right. But if I were you, I'd do the killing first. You can talk about your sins with the preacher afterwards."

Chapter 6

THEY RODE LIKE a small army over the whitening hills, Starkweather's men, a dozen of them, with Starkweather and Jack Stone in the lead. They stopped briefly at a high point and stared down into the hill-swallowed cove that was the Tundel homestead. Starkweather pulled an old army-issue telescope from his saddlebag, and extending it, peered through the lens. There was no movement anywhere in the yard, but the damage the cattle stampede had done to Tundel's cornfield and garden was in clear evidence. Scarcely a cornstalk stood that was not bent in half, the rest trampled into the ground. The same for his small orchard, branches torn away, fruit trodden into pulp. A corner of a corral had been knocked down, and the yard itself was a plowed tapestry of hoof prints. A single steer—one of Starkweather's—lay dead near the house, but no Tundel stirred.

"Maybe they're inside packing up," Jack Stone said, smirking.

"Maybe," Starkweather replied, returning the spyglass to his saddlebag. Then, with a spur and a whoop, he led his band further on.

Ward Ashmun was working his herd with the rest of his men when he spied horsemen coming his way from the east.

It was Starkweather, he knew immediately, for he believed a menacing aura hung over them wherever they went; that the shadows they cast were darker and rimmed with tremors, like the worst storm clouds.

He threw a hasty glance in the direction of his foreman and saw that Wes Bridges had seen them too. Bridges barked some orders and cowboys scattered in an attempt to slow the herd. They all knew that Starkweather never came for neighborly reasons, so Bridges quickly gathered as many riders as he could, leaving a handful to stick with the herd. All this was done with hand signals, borne out of instinct and necessity. One by one nine riders encircled their boss, all watching in readiness as Starkweather's little army came near.

"State your business," Ashmun hollered, as they drew up, getting directly to the point.

"My business is bad, Ashmun."

"When has it not?"

Starkweather's riders slowly fanned out, establishing a long line on either side of their leader. The snow was no longer falling but the wind had taken up the cry, sending swirling ribbons of snow around the legs of the horses and against the collars of the mounted men.

"You sent a man to kill my cows, Ashmun. I'm here to even the score."

"I did no such thing," Ashmun said, inwardly surprised. "I don't know what you're talking about."

"The horse is still standing in your corral. Down by your watering hole. Saddle still on him. My man tracked him there. The horse was still hot and lathered."

"When did this happen?"

"Last night."

Jack Stone was scanning Ashmun's riders. When his eyes fell on Tee Blake he nudged his horse next to Starkweather's and whispered.

"First of all, I have no interest in your cattle," Ashmun said. "And neither do my riders. We have our hands full with our own herds."

But Starkweather had stopped listening. He was looking at Blake now, his brow furrowed in confusion. Soon all eyes fell on the young cowboy.

"What in hell are you doing over there, Blake?"

Ashmun answered for him. "He rides for me."

"That's impossible."

No one moved or spoke, every Starkweather man trying to draw some sort of conclusion to this new mystery.

"I was not—" Blake started to say, but Ashmun cut him off.

"He doesn't ride for you anymore, Starkweather, so leave him be."

Starkweather and Jack Stone looked at each other.

"He's your man, then, boss," Stone said. "Before turning traitor, he probably rode up to Melgoza and went on a spree."

Slowly Starkweather edged his horse closer to the cowboy. "You're a murderer, Blake. You killed a dozen head of my cows. And two of my men. You need to hang."

"You'll do no such thing," Ashmun said.

"If he didn't do it, then who did?"

"The kid's been riding for me two days now," he lied. "And he hasn't been out of my sight. It must have been one of your other enemies. You've got plenty."

"Then explain the horse in your corral." Starkweather fumed.

"Anyone can steal a horse."

"I don't believe you, Ashmun. I don't believe a damn word you've said." Starkweather straightened up in his saddle, prompting Jack Stone to throw open his coat, revealing his two black pistols. All down the line then, riders on both sides put gloved hands on the butts of their irons. No sound was made for a full minute except the wind singing through the snowy grass.

"Are you going to turn this range into a killing field, Starkweather? Is that what you want? There's more than enough guns here for that. But whoever rides away, one thing is for certain, Starkweather—it won't be you."

Jack Stone fairly snarled. He was ready for whatever came down. More than ready.

"I want justice," Starkweather hissed.

"Then get the law."

"The law? I'm the law here."

"You might be the law on your range, Starkweather. But where you're standing right now, I am the law. This is my range and I want you off."

The two cattlemen stared at each other, fury in their eyes.

"You might be able to bully Tundel, and them other folks," Ashmun went on, "but it stops here."

"Tundel's as good as gone."

"I heard how one of your pups murdered young Junson."

"Call it what you want. Old man Tundel just lost another one. One of my riders found his oldest boy all shot to hell this morning. Pretty soon they'll all be gone. And then your range and my range will be tight up against each other."

"And then what?"

Starkweather glowered at Ashmun with black, savage eyes. "Then you might see your killing field."

"Get out," Ashmun growled.

Starkweather slowly began backing his horse away and his line of riders followed. "This isn't over," he hollered.

Jack Stone did not move. Instead he slowly inched his horse closer to where Tee Blake was. Stone let his reins hang over his saddle horn, both hands moving back to his pistols, tapping his fingers teasingly against the grips. His eyes bore into the cowboy, challenging him.

"Starkweather," Ashmun shouted. "Call off your dog."

Douglas Starkweather reined in his horse. The cords on his neck were tight as vines. His brow, filled with creases, turned black with rage. "Not today," he barked at Stone. Then he jabbed his heels into his horse's flanks and tore across the snowfield. After one last threatening stare, Jack Stone whirled his horse and galloped after his boss.

Ward Ashmun and his cowboys sat their horses in disturbed silence, watching Starkweather and his gang disappear into the snowy mist. Finally the old man's gravelly voice broke the riders out of their daze. "Well, boys, the lids off the kettle. That devil has finally made his play."

Wes Bridges turned a distrusting gaze at Blake. "What'd you know about any of this?"

"Leave it, Wes," interrupted Ashmun.

The foreman flashed anger. "But boss—"

"I said leave it," the old man growled. "Now get these cows down to the ranch. And run some scouts out on the perimeter. Starkweather is out for blood, plain enough. He won't be leaving this alone."

Bridges yanked hard on his reins. He turned to the riders and hollered bitterly for them to rejoin the herd. "Get movin', Blake."

"No," Ashmun bellowed.

Both cowboys pivoted in their saddles, showing surprise.

"I'm going to pay someone a visit. Blake, you ride with me."

A moment of confusion followed, and then Bridges whirled his horse around and pounded off after the herd.

Amos and his wife, and several of the other womenfolk, cleaned up Virgil Tundel's body. Matthew Hornfisher erected a hasty pine coffin, and clothing the dead man in a new shirt and pants, compliments of Amos's stock at the store, they placed man and coffin into the back of Matthew's buckboard. After much persuasion, Little George reluctantly agreed to ride with Matthew and Amos out to the Tundel spread.

"Please don't make me do the talkin," LG begged. "I done it once. It wouldn't be right to make me."

"Them poor folks'll be needing all the comfort we can give 'em," Amos said, patting LG on the knee. "You always have a good way for that sort of thing."

Little George let out an involuntary sob. "Just don't make me be the one to tell them."

Matthew flicked the reins and they were on their way, shotgun leaning against the seat beside him, young Tanner waving solemnly from the door of Amos' store, an ignored licorice stick in his hand.

No one spoke for the four-mile ride. LG sat in the back with Virgil's body, weeping deeply into his hands, and the snow, which had thrown its false purity across the prairie, now seemed only to add a bitter coldness to the unpleasant assignment.

As it turned out, it *was* Little George who stepped to the front of this somber group and bore to the Tundels the news of Virgil's passing. His words—so simply stated and so tenderly delivered—put such an awful stillness over them that they received his message like a eulogy. Lucy was a widow now, but she listened in tearless silence, her anger at her dead husband's rash actions, which ended predictably, outweighed her present sorrow.

The family stumbled to the wagon and lifted the coffin lid. The single wound in the wrist was shown to them, giving them a confused pause. They asked many questions, but the one question, and its answer, which brought them back to reality was—*Who brought him in?*

When Matthew said, "Brady Quinn," it was more than they could bear, and the old mother lost her legs and came to a heap on the ground.

A dry cold wind had trailed the snow and it forced Ward Ashmun and Tee Blake to follow the interior ravines to the big Ashmun house. Blake, confused at first by being asked to ride with him, understood more clearly as they rode, the old rancher peppering him with questions about Starkweather and his means of operation. Blake held nothing back, revealing the truth about his head wound, and why he was there watching the Tundel place at night in the first place.

"After today," Blake said, "I reckon it's obvious what he's after. It's like a game of chess to him, sir. The Tundel's neighbors, the ones he burned out, were just pawns. Tundel's the last of them. Begging yer pardon, Mr. Ashmun, but you are the king he wants to conquer. Tundel's just in the way."

"So it was Starkweather who ran off the Hamm brothers?"

"And the Woodsons," the cowboy said. His face turned ashen at the recollection of what he heard from Ike Werth when he returned from that raid. "It was worse than that, sir. It was murder. That's Jack Stone's part. He's Starkweather's enforcer. A man never lived that had a blacker heart."

"So you lit out," Ashmun said.

"That's not my game, Mr. Ashmun. I'm ashamed I stayed as long as I did."

They rode in silence until the ranch house came into view. The old man reined in and turned in his saddle, facing Tee Blake. "Alright," he said, his nettled voice an extension of his frustration. "What do you make of this business Starkweather threw up today?"

Blake shook his head. "I'm stumped for sure."

"No idea at all?"

"Well, I been thinking. Sort of. First off, it might be a straight lie. Might not have even happened. But sayin it did. He might have sent one of his own men to do it. Just to stir things up with you."

"You mean he'd kill his own men just to get at me."

"If he didn't, Jack Stone would do it with pleasure."

The furrows on Ward Ashmun's brow deepened.

"But then I got to thinkin about what he said. About Virgil Tundel. About him getting killed too. He didn't say where Virgil got killed. Or by who. But," Blake paused here, reluctant even to verbalize it. "But if anybody had a reason to get even with Starkweather. Well, it would be Virgil Tundel. Especially after what happened to his brother the other day."

Ashmun stroked his whiskers. "You certainly are a chess player."

"I'm jist guessing, sir. It's only a wild hunch. I sure don't want to pin a murdering on a man who can't give an answer."

Ashmun said no more. He led the way down the draw and into the big yard and once dismounted, the cowboy followed the rancher up the porch steps and through the front door. Freya Ashmun, who had heard them ride into the yard, and spied them through the window, was standing in the middle of the great room waiting for them. The anger she had leveled at her father the day before gave way to wonder when she saw the very cowboy she had turned away the night before enter through the door with him. There followed a momentary flash of secret recognition, and then a mild blush on Freya's face.

For Blake's part, he saw, in this better light of day, both her youth and her beauty.

"This here's my daughter, Freya. She believes herself the boss of this place. And honey, this is Tee Blake, my newest rider. But you better watch yourself, girl. Mister Blake here is a master chess player."

Tee Blake, with all the manners he possessed, stepped forward and extended his hand. And like a true Ashmun, she received it and shook it with earnest.

When Marshal Boone Crowe and newly reappointed deputy Rud Lacrosse rode down alongside the battered cornfield they saw three men with shovels digging a grave under a grove of bleak, leafless trees. They stopped for a moment and pitched a gaze at the damage that wracked the yard and fields. The immense swath of deep hoof prints told the story.

"I've seen this trick before," Crowe said.

"Starkweather?"

"Who else?"

Then they both looked back to the gravediggers and angled their horses in that direction. Boone recognized the father, Ernest Tundel, the back of his shirt streaked with sweat. Then he saw the storekeeper from Dry Branch and the blacksmith. Tundel stopped digging when he saw the two lawmen approach and he threw a scornful look at Boone Crowe.

"Your marshaling has come too late," he said bitterly. "I've lost two boys in three days. And Starkweather remains on his throne."

Crowe remained quiet out of respect, but Lacrosse asked what happened.

Tundel jammed his shovel in the dirt mound. "That's good and deep, fellows. I can't say how much I appreciate this," he sighed. "Let's get him down."

Lacrosse didn't wait for an answer to his question, instead quickly dismounted and took hold of a rope-end to help lower the coffin into the hole. Marshal Crowe seemed frozen in his saddle, his mind taking up distant issues. Something in the scene before him triggered a near-chocking sorrow, as if a window had opened into his own private grief, and he suddenly understood that he would never see Eva Gist alive again. It was like a reverse-epiphany, clothed in deepest dread, one he didn't want to face. But here was Ernest Tundel, forced to face his own worst dread. No matter what happened—if Starkweather could be stopped, or even killed, it could never be enough for Tundel. He'd lost two sons and nothing would bring them back. And nothing, Boone Crowe now realized, would bring Eva Gist back. He was convinced of that.

The marshal was in such a deep stupor that Lacrosse called to him twice before he was able to shake him out of his trance. "Mister Tundel asked if you would ride down to the house and escort his family up here for the burying," the deputy said, giving the old lawman a peculiar look.

Crowe stared at Lacrosse blankly, then turned Hunter without a word and headed toward the house.

It was just nearing twilight when two riders broke over the hillside to the west, riding at a casual gait. As they drew alongside what had once been the garden, they skirted it; its ruined remains trampled into the ground. The riders appeared respectful but uneasy and it wasn't until they approached the house and the strangers removed their hats that Ernest Tundel recognized Ward Ashmun.

Earlier, after words had been spoken over Virgil's grave, and after the hole had been filled in, Ernest led his family back to the outdoor fire pit in front of the house and set a pile of wood to blazing. It was a fire of rage and the ripe wood crackled and popped like a fierce and fiery battle. The flames leapt high and angry and a good bit of liberty was given the aggrieved father.

Crowe and Lacrosse stood in stupid discomfort as Amos, Matthew and LG said their sad goodbyes, and shortly old Mrs. Tundel, who had aged years in less than a week, found her bed, vowing to stay there until the Lord called her home. Lucy sat in the shadows, a stern, removed expression drawn across her handsome face. And August, who all day had remained distant and silent in his suffering, stared at Lucy through the leaping flames.

By the time Ashmun and Blake appeared in the yard, the fire had died down and the sufferers that gathered there were making valiant efforts to enjoy the coffee turning cold in their tin cups. Tundel stood like a beaten warrior and faced his visitors, half expecting more trouble, but being who he was, he greeted them respectfully.

"I've come to offer my condolences," Ashmun said, his raspy voice a welcome sound in the woeful night.

Tundel nodded.

"I admit I have not been a sympathetic neighbor," the rancher said. "You surely know the reasons. But what you have suffered is beyond any of our differences."

Boone Crowe sat on a plank bench in the evening's dimness, stunned at recognizing the young cowboy as one of Starkweather's riders, one of those present with Ike Werth just days ago when he was forced to kill their companion. He said nothing, but when Blake's eyes found the marshal the cowboy stiffened.

"Where did you get this news," Tundel asked.

"From the very mouth of Starkweather himself."

This was a shock. "You and him on sociable terms?"

"I threw him off my land."

In a few gravelly words, Ashmun told the story of their encounter. "This is hard for me, Mr. Tundel. I am a proud man, and as selfish as the rest of them. But I believe you and I have a common enemy and that somehow draws us together."

"I don't have what you have, Ashmun. But I am a proud man too. I've worked hard at what I have. And the government says I'm legal. But what you say is true. Starkweather is my enemy. I've got two graves up there to prove it," he said, jabbing his thumb in the direction of the burying hill.

Ashmun's eyes followed Tundel's gesture and for the first time noticed the two lawmen. Crowe used this as an excuse to stand.

"I'm the territorial marshal out of Buffalo. Boone Crowe's my name and I have done Mr. Tundel a terrible disservice for having not killed Starkweather back at Cold Harbor in sixty-four. I came here on my own business and neglected my duty. For that I am deeply sorry. Mr. Tundel deserved better. If I can, I plan to hang the man."

These were strange words for this meeting place. Crowe saw Lacrosse's hand go subconsciously to his throat, and through the fire's glow he saw young August Tundel nod in grave agreement.

"What do you propose," Ashmun asked.

"Starkweather is a rabid dog. And you know what we do with rabid dogs."

It was August Tundel who stood suddenly, surprising

everyone. His voice was deep. He looked at his father then at Crowe. "What about Brady Quinn? He's the one killed both Junson and Virgil. He deserves his own rope."

Blake edged his horse closer and spoke for the first time. "And Jack Stone."

Ernest Tundel stepped to August and put a comforting hand on his son's shoulder, then turned to Ashmun and Blake. "Please step down from them horses and we'll get some fresh coffee up."

Lucy stirred, welcoming a chance to be away from all this talk. "I'll get it started," she said, going through the door of the house. August watched her leave and for an instant moved to follow her, then caught himself. He offered a seat by the fire to Tee Blake, and then, with a forced courage, spoke not another word. He had said his piece already. It had been a long day that was promising to be a long night, with this, the strangest gathering of men.

The rest of the day was not kind to Brady Quinn. After riding in rage and humiliation from Dry Branch to Starkweather's ranch, he threw himself full force against the bunkhouse door, nearly springing it off its sockets, and fell upon his bunk like a scorned child. The face of the blacksmith and the words of the boy rode with him the whole way. Now, in the deserted bunkhouse, he fumed just short of tears.

I hate you. The boy's words seemed to live in his head.

The words came like birds come, circling the globe, only to come back and roost in your own trees. *I hate you.* It was one thing to deliver such venom, another to receive it. They were his words; he owned them. They were the same words he screamed at his father, following the last beating he swore he'd ever tolerate. Fourteen years old. He'd had enough. Enough of pigs and cabbages, goats, slop and drunken whippings. Two years later he robbed an old miner of his carbine and his life, and then went back home and killed his father. In a little sideways town just inside Colorado he met the only true friend he'd ever had—the Colt revolver he still carried.

It was turning dark when he heard Starkweather and his riders enter the yard, so he fled the bunkhouse, making his way among the corrals until he found a secluded place in the gloom of the hillside where it would be just him and the milky moon.

Quinn had never expected the blacksmith to show grit. Or the fearful boy at his side to find a voice. He remembered that the boy had been there when he shot Junson Tundel, the boy's frozen face a living statue of breathless fright.

Well, that's tough, he thought. Let the kid have his demons. I have my own to deal with. "I'll just have to wipe them out," he muttered to the darkness. There was no way he would let a blacksmith run him off. He would get them both if he had to. Man and boy. Just like he did the Tundels.

He found a tree and sat beneath it, forlorn as a sailor without a ship, the cold night barely penetrating his senses. The noise of the returning riders, their hoots and cavorting, mixed with the distant lowing of the herds that had been brought in earlier, finally woke him from his thoughts. They'd been out to Ashmun's range to settle a score and now he wondered how that business had been settled. But before he could ponder on this for even a moment, a new, glorious thought came to him; a thing so sudden and so satisfying that it drove the blacksmith and the boy clean from his mind.

Straightening himself up briskly, he dug his boot heels into the earth and stood, and staring open-eyed at the rising moon, he beheld there the imagined face of the daughter—Freya Ashmun.

Chapter 7

CONSCIOUSNESS CAME IN fits and starts for Ike Werth. The sun through the window was like a lance in his one good eye. His other eye remained swelled tight as a cellar door. He blinked in dumb wonder at his surroundings, knowing not where he was, or remembering for a spell, about why he was here. When recollection did filter through he fumbled for a while putting the pieces together. Lifting his head from the pillow was its own torture; the sharp hammer blows of pain nearly causing him to pass out.

On his feet he staggered to a mirror hanging on the wall and inspected the damage. A gruesome ogre stared back; the ringed imprint of a horseshoe left its perfect tattoo red and ugly on his broken cheek and jaw. Outside the window, on the boardwalk, he could hear the doctor talking, giving a lesson to some citizen on setting a broken arm. *Something between a meaningful jerk and a compassionate yank*. It made no sense.

Ike scanned the room for his hat and pistol belt, fighting back the nausea. He wrestled his coat on too, then, trying to keep a steady footing, ambled through the door. The snow of the day before had been driven away in the night by a warm wind and by this present sunshine, turning the streets to mud.

"Whoa there, fella," Dr. Wills said. "I'm not sure you're fit to be on your feet."

"Horsh…ma…horsh." Ike's words floated crazily with

his unhinged jaw.

The doctor shrugged, then pointed down the street to the livery stable, the very scene of Ike's malady, and the battered man lumbered off.

"Ain't he gonna pay up?" the citizen asked.

"Already did. Paid in advance out of his own wallet."

"But…"

Doc Wills winked, and then patted his own vest pocket.

In a few minutes, the two men saw Ike Werth, barely upright in his saddle, his face a picture of wretched scorn, ride out of Fort Tillman with a look neither left nor right, his horse throwing up clods of mud in its wake.

Marshal Crowe and deputy Lacrosse emerged from Tundel's barn where they had spent the night and proceeded to the pump to wash up. August Tundel was already up and moving around the yard, making preparations to butcher the dead Starkweather steer that he had killed during the stampede. Meat was meat, and too many more days would see it spoiled. Two brothers dead but life goes on.

"You men fixin to leave out now?" August said without looking up, yet showing no bitterness.

"Only for a spell," Boone answered. "I want to ride up the valley here and make a survey of those two other homesteads. The ones that got burned out. Are they far?"

"Not far. Hamm's place only three miles. Woodson's

three or four past that."

Lacrosse palmed handfuls of water through his hair then shook like a dog. He pulled his hat on over his wet hair then strode to the barn to bring out the horses.

"How is your mother this morning?" Boone asked.

"Same as yesterday. She's taken to her bed, you know."

"I'm sorry to hear that. And your brother's wife?"

No sooner had he spoken these last words then Lucy Tundel appeared through the door of the house carrying a passel of utensils for butchering the slain animal. Her hair was pulled back behind her head, with several loose strands circling like coils of thread around her temples. She had on a man's coat—probably Virgil's—and her face was set in a cast of willful compulsion. She would see these tragic events through on her own terms and taking to her bed, like Ma Tundel had done, would not be one of them.

August moved to her side, taking one of the kettles from her and together they began sorting through the knives and bone cutters and varied slaughtering apparatus. They would butcher it where it lay, taking what they wanted, much the way the Indians had done when bison were plentiful. Boone Crowe watched them working, side-by-side, their shoulders touching sometimes, laboring in silent communication. Crowe watched with a flame of envy, thinking of Eva and what he and she might have shared.

Lacrosse returned with the saddled horses and they rode out without a further word. The snow had disappeared in the night and the two lawmen stuck to the sunny ridges to avoid getting mired down in soft soil. They had scarcely ridden a half hour when the charred frame of a torched barn made its ugly impression on the hillside. Not far from it was the house where Chester and Lance Hamm had once tried to scratch out a new life for themselves. Weeds and wild grass had savaged the yard and corrals had been pulled down, presumably by Starkweather's men. The doorway to the cabin, where the one brother had died, still stood open and as they rode through the desolate yard a coyote suddenly darted from the dank opening, racing wildly into the brush. The two men looked at each other but said nothing.

In another hour, they were watering their horses in a small, nameless creek that ran through the deserted Woodson farm. This barn, like the Hamm's barn, leaned like a dejected skeleton against itself, the blackened timbers like a tabletop of scattered dominos. The three graves, dug by Ernest and Virgil Tundel, already showed signs of invasion by badgers and snakes. Three graves. The husband, the wife and the daughter.

Old man Tundel, when the marshal had stopped by the first time, away from his own house and even then with a hushed, sickened voice, gave Crowe a description of what the two women looked like when he and Virgil found them.

I'm not a drinking man, Tundel had said. *But after we buried them folks, I went out in my barn that night and drank myself into a stupor. Only an animal could do that to a woman. Much less a girl.*

While Lacrosse kicked through the debris in the yard, the marshal dismounted and walked to the little house. He planned to go in, to look around, to fetch up evidence, but a freezing chill suddenly overtook him. It ran down his neck like a live thing, and his face grew abruptly cold, as if he had fallen into a frozen lake. He reached for the door latch but then pulled back, recoiling from some dark invisible force. Turning to see if Lacrosse had noticed any of this, and realizing he had not, he quickly moved back to Hunter and returned to his saddle. He pulled off his hat and touched a palm to his forehead. It was not cold like he expected, rather wet with a troubled sweat.

The devil has been here, he thought. The devil and the devil's apprentice.

"We better get back to Tundel's place," he said, shakily. "I've a strong feeling Starkweather's planning a visit. And I want to be there when he does."

"Me too," said Lacrosse, nodding in agreement. "That's my hunch too."

"Tundel ought to be beaten now," Starkweather said. "That Quinn boy has done a pretty good job of whittling them down." He and Jack Stone stood beneath the tattered Confederate flag that hung on the wall of the big house. "But I want insurance. Tundel's a tough old nut. I wouldn't be surprised if he still stuck it out. May figure he hasn't much else to lose."

"You thinking of another barn burning?" Stone asked, the familiar sardonic smile rising across his face.

"The barn *and* the house. I want him leveled. I don't care if you have to burn them all. I'm sick of that stubborn old coot standing between Ashmun and me."

"Then what about Ashmun?"

This drew an agitated look from Starkweather. "You worry about Tundel, Jack. I'll handle Ashmun. He thinks he got something on us yesterday, but he's mistaken. He's not prepared for the kind of fight I'm thinking of."

Starkweather moved to a desk and retrieved two black cigars from a case. Both men leaned into a lighted match then exhaled clouds of leaden smoke. "Take five or six men into Dry Branch. Go right now. Let em drink up some courage."

Jack Stone, stroking the ends of his yellow Texas bandana, nodded approvingly.

A clamor of curious activity came from the courtyard and both men went out onto the front porch, where a group of men were gathered around a single man on horseback. Several of them were helping the man down and Starkweather was surprised to see Ike Werth teetering on weak legs, his whiskered face showing a sagging jaw. Ike looked up and stumbled to the porch where he promptly collapsed on the top step.

"Get him inside," the boss hollered, and another group scrambled to his aid.

Once lying on a couch, his spurred boots hanging off the side, Starkweather knelt and looked closely at the scarred, swollen face.

"What the hell happened?"

"Ah…horsh…kit…me."

Starkweather untangled the bandana from around Ike's neck and lifting his jaw upward, wrapped the bandana vertically over his face, securing the broken jaw in place. "You should have done that from the first. Now talk slow. I can't understand a damn word you're saying."

In a broken slur, Ike related what he found on the boardwalk of Fort Tillman—the corpse of Milo Clemons. He said that he checked around. Found out it was that very same deputy that they nearly hung a spell back. And that marshal was with him.

"Crowe?"

Ike nodded.

"Is he still there?"

Ike shrugged. Then nodded.

"What happened to your face?"

Ike's eyes lit with fire. "It…wash the…marsa'l's bay. I'm gon kill tat hoss…then the marsa'l."

"You're a fool, Ike. That old duck is nobody to mess with. You'll end up like Milo."

Jack Stone grunted and Starkweather turned and gave him a cautionary look. Stone ignored the warning with his usual sneer.

"Get your men and head into town," Starkweather said. "Tonight's the night. And Ike. You better stick around the bunkhouse for a while. You're too ugly to look at."

The party broke up and the men lifted Ike off the couch, but as they reached the door Starkweather spoke again. "On second thought, Ike. I have a job for you. Leave him here boys and get back to work."

They all left, Jack Stone with them, leaving only the boss and Ike Werth alone.

"Can you sit a horse?"

Werth nodded uncertainly.

"You'll need a rifle and a fresh horse."

He nodded again.

"And this." Starkweather stepped to a cabinet and taking out a bottle of whisky filled a glass and handed it to Ike. "Can you aim that down your throat without making a mess?"

Ike took the whisky and with the caution and care of a surgeon drained the glass, only a small drop falling from his beard.

"Now listen. Your old pard Blake has turned traitor. He jumped to Ashmun's side. I want him dead by morning. Understand?"

Werth's face clouded with surprise but after a moment he nodded consent.

"Good. Have another whisky."

Wes Bridges stood impatiently beside the buckboard waiting for Freya Ashmun and her girl, Yuridia to emerge from the house. Ashmun had instructed him to ride in to Dry Branch and pick up a list of supplies from Amos Bright's store. With the cattle back grazing close to home now, it would mean more hands eating everyday grub instead of the usual beans and flour biscuits of the upper ranges. Wes welcomed the break in routine, and especially the opportunity to have the daughter ride along. But then Freya insisted that Yuridia come. Then, too, at the last minute Ashmun told Tee Blake to escort them on horseback. That turned Bridges' temper sour. He did not understand how this damn Starkweather rider had found such sudden favor with the old man. The possibility of a pleasant ride with Freya had turned into a clown's parade.

When the two young women finally showed themselves, the blonde, pretty Freya climbed up onto the seat next to Wes Bridges while Yuridia, in her own dark, contrasting beauty, sat in the back. Blake, already in his saddle, tipped his hat to both women, whereupon they acknowledged him with a smile.

Wes Bridges spit out a whoop to the harnessed horses and with a flick of the reins they were on their way.

Across the open land, a band of seven riders crossed the last narrow valley before dipping down into Dry Branch, Jack Stone, Ethan Moss and Brady Quinn among them. Tanner Hornfisher saw them come up, the noonday sun at their back, and he retreated into the shadows of his father's blacksmith shop. The billows were still and airless and the fire but a quiet bed of sleeping embers because Matthew Hornfisher was not there. Tanner stood in the center of the room, facing the open front door, his eyes fixed with a hatred black as the anvil that stood beside him.

The riders clomped boldly down the street two abreast, taking in the place with curious stares, as if it was their first time there. Jack Stone led the way to Clive Leyland's saloon and motioned with a nod of his head for the rest to follow. They tied their horses at the rails all along the street front and stepped up onto the duckboard walk, all except Brady Quinn. He had lingered at the blacksmith shop, peering into its dim interior, his right hand resting near his Colt.

"Boss wants your courage up," Jack Stone hollered. "Better get in here."

"I don't drink," Quinn said, over his shoulder, his eyes still piercing the vacant smithy shop.

"Your horse throw a shoe or something?" Stone asked.

"He's looking for trouble, don't you know," Ethan Moss said. "It's true he doesn't drink. He gets his thrills from other things."

"Like what?"

Ethan wanted to say—*he's not that much different than you, Stone*. But he held his tongue and simply shrugged. Both men turned then and followed the other riders into the saloon.

Outside Brady Quinn nudged his horse closer to the doorway and standing stiffly in the middle of the dirt floor, he spied the boy.

"Well, I'll be. If it ain't the boy who hates me." He said this, feinting bravado, but inwardly he was unnerved by the boy's lack of visible fear. Quinn looked around then and seeing no one else, said, "Is yer daddy hiding somewhere."

Tanner said nothing.

"Well, he's not much of a dad to leave you here to face down the bad guys all alone. He must be somewhere."

The boy's head lifted and his chin aimed itself defiantly at the gunman. But his eyes betrayed him, as he let them rotate ever so slightly for a brief second towards a place beyond the door.

Quinn followed Tanner's eyes, turning his head and looking where the boy was looking. At first he saw nothing but the empty street and the horses tied to the hitching rails. But then, gazing further, he saw where cemetery hill rose above the town, and there, amongst the tombstones and the scattered sage bushes, stood a lone man.

"Well, well," Quinn said, backing his horse out of the doorway. He patted his pistol fondly and then giving his horse a spur, trotted down the street and upwards to cemetery hill. Tanner sucked in his breath and then sped after him on foot.

Matthew Hornfisher was standing in front of a headstone holding a weak bouquet of prairie grass, burnt reddish-yellow by the late autumn wind. It was too late in the season for proper flowers but he did what he could with what he had. He heard the horse approaching behind him and guessed at who it was because he had seen the seven riders on the horizon earlier. But there was nothing to be done about it, he knew.

"What a charming picture," the gunman said. He dismounted and let the reins fall to the ground.

Matthew turned slowly, bending and placing the

bouquet at the foot of the gravestone, then stood, facing the young killer.

"You don't seem happy to see me," Quinn said. "Shame yer boy ain't here to protect you this time."

"What'd you want? We don't need your trouble here."

"You're in a friendly mood. Why, I jist come up here to pay my respects to these poor dead folks." He began making a wide circle amongst the graves, walking across them disrespectfully, sifting the mounded dirt with the toe of his boot.

Tanner had finally made it to within a hundred feet of the cemetery when his father hollered at him to stop. "Stay there, Tanner. I mean it. Not a step closer."

With great difficulty the boy obeyed.

Behind the boy came another horseman. It was Ethan Moss. He passed Tanner and rode directly up to where the gunman's horse stood.

"I want you down off here, Quinn," Moss said.

"Whad're you buttin in for. This feller and I have a beef to settle. Ain't that right, Mr. Blacksmith Man?"

"Maybe so, but it won't be what you want," the foreman said.

"And what's that, Moss."

"A killing. Not here. Not like this."

"And why not."

"Don't be stupid, Quinn. You'd hang. He's unarmed. And I'd testify against you with a smile on my face."

"I can't leave him off."

Hornfisher listened to this exchange in weighty silence.

He knew now what Quinn's intention had been all along. To murder him. The same way he'd done to the Tundel brothers.

"I've always been curious, Quinn," Moss said.

"About what?"

"I've always been curious what kind of man you'd be without that hogleg of yours. This here just might be the time to find out."

"Whad're you sayin?"

"You know what I'm saying. Unhitch that gun belt and show us what you've got."

"You want me to fight this guy?"

"You're doin a lot of talking, Quinn."

For the first time, the gunman looked into Matthew Hornfisher's face and what he saw there was a strange resolve. He wanted desperately to pull his Colt from its holster and put a bullet in him, but instead, with unsteady fingers, he unfastened his gun belt and let it slide to the ground. Doubling his hands into tight fists he stepped forward to face his enemy.

Matthew stood still, arms at his sides, veins throbbing at his temples. "You're standing on my wife's grave," he hissed.

Stupidly, Quinn glanced down at his feet. Matthew moved in swiftly and smashed a hard fist against the gunman's forehead, knocking him off his feet and onto his back. Stunned, Quinn laid there long enough for Matthew to land a boot deep into his ribs.

Tanner remained where he was but his tongue had found

his lips and it was circling them with great vigor. Moss too, watched with curious pleasure.

Matthew Hornfisher pulled Quinn to his feet by his shirt and wrapping his arm tight around the gunman's head and proceeded to deliver punch after punch to his nose and chin. Blood was flowing now and Matthew pushed the battered Quinn away. They stood facing each other, Quinn already worn out. He spit blood into the dirt and then with a bobbing head scanned the ground for his pistol. Seeing it he took one step towards it but Matthew's fist connected hard behind Quinn's right ear and he fell to the ground, face in the damp muck.

Matthew picked up Quinn's gun belt and handed it to Moss. "You keep this away from him. I have a double barrel shotgun in my shop. If he even looks at me again I'll cut him in half."

Moss took the gun and holster and watched as Matthew Hornfisher moved to his son's side, and putting his arm around the boy's shoulder, walked him down the hill.

They moved away from the north now, back towards the Tundel homestead, but by a different route. Lacrosse had seen a grove of cottonwoods, fed by the small nameless creek that had meandered through what was left of the Woodson farm. He was trying to find the tree where Starkweather's men had come upon him that fateful day of his hanging, but as they drew near he realized it was not the place.

"Too far east," he said. "And I don't remember the creek being this close to the trees."

"Creeks rise and fall," Boone said. "There's probably a dozen little groves like this within ten miles."

"Probably." The deputy tipped his hat back and gazed in all directions, trying to get his bearings. They were a hundred yards from the grove now, riding slow.

"Why is it so all-fired important to find that same tree? You planning to cut it down or something?"

"I never thought of that. If I find it, I think I might just—"

The horse fell to its knees before they heard the shot and Lacrosse scrambled hurriedly out of the saddle to keep the wounded animal from rolling over on him. Boone Crowe was out of the saddle and pulling Hunter down into a flattened position. They were out in the open with no cover but as he pulled the hidden pistol from under his coat he saw a puff of smoke from a second shot. A rifle, he knew. Coming from the cottonwoods.

"We can't stay here," Crowe hollered, firing into the grove.

Lacrosse's horse took another bullet, and it gave off a dying moan. The deputy pulled his Winchester from the saddle scabbard, and levering in a shell, he fired three successive shots into the trees. Both men lay behind the dead horse now, their heads down.

"I think there's just one of them," Crowe said. "But that's just a guess."

Lacrosse was pale with rage. Another shot threw up dirt only inches from Hunter's head. Both lawmen looked at each other. "Horses first, looks like," Crowe said. "That won't stand. How many shells in that Winchester?"

"Five maybe. I've got more in the saddle bags."

"Watch for his smoke. Then start pouring in the lead. I'll get Hunter up as fast as I can and we'll give him a full frontal charge. If you can keep him pinned down I might be able to get close enough to root him out. If you see him at all, nail him."

"That's too risky, Boone."

"We got no choice. Look around. We're on the flat. We can't circle on him. Count to three, then start shooting. And for pity sake, aim straight. I don't want you shooting me. Now count."

By the time he reached three Hunter was up and the marshal leapt into the saddle in the fashion of an Indian, moving faster than Lacrosse thought an old man could move. He rose up and began laying down a covering fire.

Boone Crowe rode hard and fast, reaching the halfway mark before pulling his pistol again and firing. He prayed that Hunter would not be harmed in this idiotic tactic. He could hear Lacrosse's Winchester bark twice, then three times but he had not seen any firing from the trees. Riding full out he emptied the first pistol then shoving it back under his coat, pulled the Colt from its holster and fired twice more. Almost there, he suddenly saw a figure dart from one tree to the next and then stumble in mid-step and roll like a ball on the ground. Crowe was out of the saddle now, pulling Hunter deeper into the thick grove, hoping to conceal the animal. Crouching, he moved to his left, wanting to come upon the fallen figure from behind. Lacrosse had stopped firing. The wind in the brittle leaves was the only sound.

Then he saw the figure rise up in front of him and he shot twice, throwing the man backwards. Boone closed on him quickly, ready to shoot again. The ambusher was lying on his side, hands empty, blood in great abundance, leaking from his side and from his neck.

"You alone?"

The shot man spit a stringy glob of blood at Crowe.

The marshal considered the man, saw the closed eye, the horseshoe tattoo on his face, and could hardly believe he was looking at Ike Werth. "I left you only yesterday. Stretched on a hard bed at the doc's office. You made a bad choice by coming here."

Lacrosse was coming across the meadow cautiously, rifle cocked and ready. "What'd you got there, Boone?"

"You better come and see for yourself. You may not believe it."

Rud Lacrosse came into the grass and the trees and looked down at Ike. He shook his head. "That horse kick musta made you plum loco. You come ridin a long way just to get kilt."

"You're bleeding to death, Ike. Where you fixin to go from here?"

"Too bad the one-armed preacher ain't here," Lacrosse said.

"How in the hell did you know we were going to be here," Crowe wanted to know.

Ike was sinking now. The fury had left him along with most of his blood and he laid still. "Jus..luch."

"Luck, huh. Well, it was damn poor luck if you ask me. I should have killed you days ago and saved you the trouble."

"And I'd still have a horse if you had," Lacrosse said. Then he pulled off his bandana and knelt down in front of the doomed rider. "Remember this, Ike. See this ugly scar on my once beautiful neck. That was you. Holdin the rope. Funny how things work out though, ain't it. Me here and you there."

Ike blinked. "Fun…*ny*."

"We won't be burying you," Crowe said. "Just so you know that. We've got to be on our way. And now that we're a horse shy, we'll have to snag yours. If you're really lucky, Ike, you might meet some of your friends in hell by tonight."

Ike Werth was dead by the time they gathered their gear. They found the dead man's horse tied back in the deep brush of the grove. They took Ike's rifle and pistol and all the ammunition they could find. "If Starkweather strikes soon, we'll need all the firepower we can get."

Pulling his saddle and bridle from his killed horse, Lacrosse transferred his gear onto Ike's. As they rode together towards Tundel's again, the two lawmen marveled at how their paths had crossed with the outlaw. "Preacher would have called that divine intervention," Lacrosse said.

"I reckon," said the marshal.

"Quinn never knew which end was up," Ethan Moss soliloquized to his audience of drinkers at the bar. "Take away that fancy pistol and that boy's a regular lamb."

"What was he doing messin around with the blacksmith fer anyway," the rider Dibbs said. "Anyone makes a livin wrestling with the hind legs of a horse ain't nobody to fool with."

"Maybe we need to pay this blacksmith a visit," Jack Stone said.

Moss shook his head. "I say we let him be. He ain't done nothing wrong. 'Cept give that pup a deserved whipping."

"Where's Quinn now."

"He's sittin on the back stoop watchin the sun go down. And nursing a sore head."

Jack Stone glanced over at Leyland who was in a far corner of the bar wiping beer glasses with a towel. Leyland had not forgotten the last time Jack Stone had come to town, so he was making himself as invisible as possible, praying that there would be no gun play this time.

The gunslinger questioned if he should even take Quinn on this little fire party tonight. Granted, he needed more than just a bunch of noisemakers to do this job, which was what most of these cowpunchers were. What he needed was killers and Quinn was that for sure. But he didn't like the kid. And he didn't trust him. And then there was the woman. Virgil's poor widow woman. He'd spied her through the telescope more than once while lying up on the hill. She was a handsome one. He didn't want anything or anybody getting in the way of that.

Moss saw the dark shadow move across Stone's face, saw his black mood rising. He'd seen it before and knew the things that were coming. Ethan Moss never disobeyed orders. He didn't always like them, but times were getting tough for cowpunchers these days and he wanted to keep his job. He would do what he had to do, but he didn't have to think about it all day long. When they rode in with torches tonight, then he could think about it—not now. Looking up he motioned for Leyland to bring another bottle of courage-maker to their table.

Wes Bridges stopped the buckboard at the edge of town and stared down the street.

"This is not good," he said. "Those are Starkweather horses, ain't they, Blake?"

"Yup," he said. "That second one there, the paint. That's Jack Stone's."

"What's your call?"

"Quinn's horse is there too."

"You think they mean trouble," Freya asked. A week ago she would have laughed off such caution, but after having seen Junson gunned down in the street by Brady Quinn, she had a new sense of prudence.

"It'll be trouble alright," Blake said.

"So, what're you figurin?" Bridges asked again.

"Well, you know they'd like to put me down. That's a sure thing. I doubt they'll hurt the gals. But I can't be certain. I've heard stories about Stone."

"What stories," asked Freya.

Blake did not answer. Instead he turned to Bridges. "What would Ashmun expect us to do?"

The foreman shook his head. "He's never run away from a fight in his life."

"I had a feeling you'd say that."

They remained where they were for several more minutes saying nothing. Finally Wes Bridges said, "You keep back. Wait for us here by these houses."

"You're telling me to hide."

"I'm telling you to stay alive. If you're right, and they make trouble with you, then it'll be trouble for all of us. They may not say anything much to me. You, they might kill. We'll be as quick as we can."

"I don't like it."

"You got a better idea?"

Freya looked up at Blake and gave him a reaffirming nod. "Do what Wes says. Please."

It was the *please* that swayed him. "Alright. But the first sign of trouble, I'm coming in."

And then Freya added, "Yuridia. You stay with him. I would never have brought you if I'd have known there might be danger."

The Mexican girl did not argue. Scooting herself off the buckboard she moved to where Blake and his horse stood.

Bridges looked at them, and then giving the reins a flip,

jerked the wagon forward.

Tee Blake dismounted. He looked at the girl, considering her, and then concealed her and himself behind a granary, keeping a sharp eye out as the buckboard stopped in front of Amos Bright's store. He watched Bridges help Freya down and usher her inside. He expected to hear shouting, or shooting, but hardly a noise came from either the store or the adjoining saloon.

Inside, Wes Bridges handed Amos the list that Ashmun had given him. Their eyes met and the unstated-threat was recognized between them.

"Let's just get the basics," Wes said. "Half the flour for now. We can get more later. But we'll need the sugar and coffee and this other stuff."

Amos turned to his wife for help in gathering the supplies and the two of them sprang into action. Freya, upon entering, lingered by the door. She had hoped to look at Amos's catalogs but instead fingered a display of china cups by the front window. Through the opening that separated the two establishments drifted the low rumble of rough conversation. Glasses clanked and an occasional whoop leaked through the doorway.

Bridges carried a big sack of flour out to the buckboard. When he came back in for another sack he saw Jack Stone standing in the store, his ugly six-guns gleaming in the dimming lantern light.

"Well, isn't this just sweet," Stone said. "Old Leyland brought us in a gal after all. If that don't beat all. Maybe he can scare up a piano player."

Freya stood perfectly still, failing to mask her revulsion.

"How about it, honey. Let me buy you a drink."

"I don't think so," Bridges said.

"I wasn't talking to you, cowboy."

Bridges stiffened. Then more faces appeared behind Stone, some of them wearing drunken grins. Finally Ethan Moss moved to the front and stood beside Jack Stone.

"Well…if it ain't Ashmun's bulldog," he said, his voice lapsed in a whisky slur. "You courtin the bossh's daughter these days."

"Shut your mouth," Freya said.

"Whoa," Stone said. "She's a regular wildcat. How's she ride?"

Freya moved toward the dark gunman, her hand raised to slap his face, but Bridges stepped in front of her. "That'll do," he whispered. "Get in the wagon. Turn it around and head out of town."

"I will not."

"A regular lover's quarrel," Stone laughed. "Take note, boys. I can see who the boss of that ranch is."

Pushing his way in through the crowd of cowboys came Brady Quinn, his face showing a landscape of welts and bruises. "What's this…"

Moss patted him on the shoulder. "Bridges here is stealin your gal, Brady."

The kid's hand moved instinctively to his hip but there was no gun there.

"Easy does it, boy," Stone said, grinning. "We got work to do tonight."

This remembered information silenced the room. Dibbs spoke up. "Sun's droppin alright."

"Well, pretty lady. I guess I'll have to take a rain check on that dance." Stone turned to his riders. "Get your last drink, boys. There's work ahead."

All but Moss turned back into the saloon. He stood facing Bridges, heat rising between them.

"I got nothing to say to you, Moss. You're half drunk." Bridges turned then and began carrying more supplies out to the buckboard. Amos, trying to control his trembling hands, pitched in. His wife had long ago fled into the backroom. Freya, turning her back on Moss, walked outside and stood on the boardwalk.

When the wagon was loaded, Bridges helped Freya back in and taking up the reins, turned the team back up to where Blake waited with the Mexican girl. Halfway to the granary, Bridges realized that Ethan Moss was following them on foot. Stopping the wagon, he stepped down and the two men faced each other in the growing twilight.

"What is it you want, Moss? You've had your bad fun. No one got hurt. Why not call it off."

"I'll be in yer place someday, Bridges."

"What's that supposed to mean?"

"It means…yer days up on that big hill are 'bout…over."

"You're whiskied-up, Ethan. Go home."

Drunk or not, Moss's hand moved to his pistol and with a single motion fired. Stunned, Bridges drew too and fired. Moss staggered, then dropped to his knees. He stayed like that, his face contorted in pain. He still gripped his pistol so

Bridges stayed at the ready. By now Starkweather's men were pouring out of the saloon and running towards them, pistols out.

Jack Stone came up first. "What in *thee* hell. You just killed our foreman."

"He drew on me."

Moss was resting on his haunches now, breathing heavily, a blossom of blood just beginning to appear in the middle of his gut. He looked down at his pistol and then let it drop to the ground. "*He's*…he's right…Jack. I pulled…on him."

"Why did you do a fool thing like that?"

"I'm tired. *Ta*..take me home."

Jack Stone looked at Bridges then at Freya, who still sat on the buckboard seat, her face drawn and pale. Then he turned to his riders. "Saddle up. Saddle up now. Quinn. Come here. Get Moss up on a horse and deliver him back to Starkweather."

Quinn looked at Moss then back to Stone. "He can't ride no horse. Look at him."

"You heard what I said."

"But what about—"

"Shut up."

Bridges backed away. Climbing onto the bench seat, he flicked the reins and the wagon moved ahead, leaving Starkweather's men to sort out the rest of their night. At the granary, he stopped and Blake helped Yuridia into the back, then tying his horse to the wagon box, he sat down beside the Mexican girl and the whole rig disappeared into the night.

Chapter 8

THE MOON ROSE like a trembling oath and for a time Boone Crowe was afraid to look at it, fearing it might look back with an accusing face. He was no longer marshaling. Now he was a hunter—a tracker on the trail of a desperately deranged animal. Starkweather's craze for empire was causing problems and Crowe knew now that he had to play it like the war it was. He sat in the loft of the Tundel's barn staring through the window at a moon he never expected to see. With yesterday's snow, and a threat of rain only hours ago, the creamy circle rolled out from behind the clouds after all and now stood in the night sky like a frosty omen.

"That was a good speech you gave the Tundels." It was Lacrosse, directly below Crowe, guarding the main door of the barn.

"I'm not much for speechifying."

"Well, it was a fine one. Told them what they needed to know."

"What? Shoot to kill. That's not much of a speech."

"You jarred 'em good, though. Telling them that this would be the fight for their lives."

"Humph. That's pretty bare advice for a family just lost two boys in a week."

"Stop being so negative."

"I'm not being negative," Crowe grunted. "I just don't want any more harm coming to them. They expected me to do something before. Instead I was off chasing a fool's dream."

Lacrosse understood where this was going and let it drop. After a quiet spell he said, "You seem pretty sure Starkweather'll come tonight."

"I do. Tonight or tomorrow night. He's not one to waste much time. He figures Tundel's broke up. Now he plans to bury him. Either way, I'm sticking until he strikes. He's been at this game too long."

"Tell me about Cold Harbor. You mentioned it a couple of times."

"I don't want to."

"Was Starkweather there?"

"We were all there. The whole damn world was there."

"I thought you were with Thomas at Chickamauga."

"I was there too. That was before. They moved me out from under Thomas and sent some of us to Virginia. That's when we did Grant's dirty work at Cold Harbor."

"So, if Starkweather was a Johnny Reb, how did you know he was there?"

"Why don't you read a book about it, Rud? I'm not much for reliving it, if you don't mind."

After a long pause, Lacrosse spoke again. "Well, I hope tonight ends it."

"Shoot straight and it will."

"Who'd you reckon got old Ike?"

"Probably you," Crowe said, disinterestedly.

"He was hit twice."

"I know that. But I think you did it. Why's it so all-fired important?"

"You oughta remember. Ike was pulling on the rope that hung me. It's just kind of satisfying knowing I evened up the score."

"Congratulations. It doesn't always work out that way."

"What'd you make of these folks? Think that kid August has grit?"

"He'll do fine."

"What about the old man?"

"He fought somewhere. I forget where he said. He's got more reason to fight tonight than any of us. He'll be ready."

"And the woman? The young one?"

Women, Crowe thought. What do I know about women?

All over this part of Wyoming, other eyes were watching the moon. Wes Bridges, unable to rest, could not understand what provoked Ethan Moss to act so irrational. Blake told him on the tense ride home that Moss was generally not a very violent man. *Maybe he had a long time grudge on you.* Over what? *People do strange things.* The whisky didn't seem enough. If Moss was not a particularly violent man, he wasn't much for the bottle either. Maybe it was just written somewhere in some heavenly book or something that Ethan Moss would die today and such things had to come to pass, sensible or not.

Bridges didn't know—figured he never would. But friend or foe, he was sorry he had to be the one to do it.

Freya Ashmun stood alone in her bedroom. She had parted the curtains and was staring through the window at the same moon, brooding over the mystery of life. And something had come about today that mystified it further. She and Bridges gave a report to her father about what had happened and after a bout of his usual rage, and vexing oaths directed at Starkweather, at bad damn luck, and finally at himself for letting them go in the first place, he settled into a pacing machine, crossing from one end of the large living room to the next on a quest to wear out the carpet, vexed by what Starkweather might do when he found out that his beloved foreman got killed by his own foreman.

But Freya wondered if it was something in the telling. Or was it before that? Was it on the ride back to the ranch? A light, where there had been no light before. Like a door opening. Everything was suddenly clearer. Whatever *everything* was. She was young, but unexpectedly not as young as yesterday, not as young even as this morning. Things had changed. She seemed to be balancing between being hot and cold. And of course, that was a poor explanation too. Could it have been an odor? The smell of cattle? The leather of Wes Bridges' chaps? His boots. Or was it the lingering smoke from his pistol. Or was it…was it just *him*?

But Ethan Moss was not dead, not yet. He had coughed and sputtered in the saddle for two miles, until Quinn, who was riding a little ahead, heard the foreman fall to the ground. Dismounting, he dragged the fallen man to a cleft in the trail and laid him down.

"You will not make it, Ethan. You should have stayed back there," he said, motioning toward town. "I can try and take you back if you want."

"No. This'll do."

Brady Quinn walked around in the darkness, kicking at clumps of wild grass, impatient for this to end so he could be on his way, alone. "You in pain?"

"Yes."

Quinn looked down at him. "Why'd you say that about Bridges makin time with my gal? I have no gal."

"I heard…you and Junson Tundel…fought over her once. I figured that's…why you kilt him."

"Hell, I don't know. Maybe it was?"

"She's a…*cough*…"

"Don't talk no more. You need to stop talkin."

They were quiet for a while, Quinn stomping around in the grass and Moss laboring at his breathing. Finally he said, "Look at that moon, Quinn. That's…a lover's moon."

Quinn stopped his tramping and looked up. "I wouldn't know much about that."

"It's…*cough*…it's the kind of moon you…*cough*…kiss yer girl under."

The young cowboy looked up again, studying the

luminous ball, and tried to imagine what it would be like if such a thing was true, about kissing a gal, about even having a gal.

"That's why the...the blacksmith nearly...*cough*...kilt you today. You was standin on his...*cough*...dead wife's grave. That's what...makes him better than us, Quinn. He...he knew how to...*cough*...how to...love someone..."

Brady Quinn did not like the truth of that. It was as painful as the boy, telling him he hated him. He thought about Jack Stone and the stories he had heard from Ike and the others about what Jack thought women were good for—the *only* thing they were good for. But what Moss was saying now, about moons and gals and love, was different from what Jack Stone did. Still, he wondered—had always wondered—what it would be like to kiss Freya Ashmun. What it would be like to put a hand on her shoulder. Or to let his fingers put touches to her face.

He turned back to the foreman. "Did you ever have a gal, Ethan? Did you ever sit under a moon like this and kiss yer gal?"

But Ethan Moss had no more answers left in him.

The blind, mute Indian called Coyote knew the moon was high even though he couldn't see it. Having seen it most of his life he knew what it looked like. But even now he could feel its presence—it is how his people measured time, measured seasons. It gave its own air to the night world.

Coyote knew there had been trouble in the town today. He could feel it. He could sense the closeness of the *bad-man*. He heard their voices in the drinking place, and later the two guns making their fire. The boy came to be with him later, his very nearness as pleasing as moving water. His chirpy voice as calming as crickets. A strong boy, strangely older than his ten snows. But, some young boys are like that.

But now Coyote was alone. Alone with his sightless knowledge that the moon was out and that the stars were hanging in the sky alongside it.

The raiders came with their torches already flaming, the heavy sound of men and horses pounding the dark earth, a flaming cavalcade descending the hill. There were not seven of them anymore, with the absence of Moss and Quinn, only five, but Stone felt confident even five was plenty. He figured Tundel, taken by surprise, would cow down in his little house when the first shots were fired. And it was Jack Stone's private scheme to ride right up to the door of that little house, burst in, kill the men before they knew what was happening, and take the woman. It had worked many times in Texas, and even a few times here. It would work again.

But what the raiders rode into was a hail of bullets, from both the barn and the house. Two of the raiders fell outright, their horses rearing and pitching their shot bodies onto the ground. Torches were instantly thrown down. Stone and Nibbs had ridden directly to the house and now were caught in a hot crossfire. The third rider, abandoning all care, tried to retreat back up the hill but he was riding squarely in the circle of the moon and a shot from Lacrosse's Winchester pitched him forward onto his saddle horn where he slumped, arms dangling.

Suddenly the long barrel of Ernest Tundel's shotgun penetrated a crack in the door, and with a roar, buckshot tore through the neck of Jack Stone's mount. The horse screamed, threw its head back and then collapsed. Stone came off on his feet. The whole night had turned into furious chaos. He saw Nibbs beside him, and called out.

"No!" Nibbs shouted, trying to control his own mount, which was in a panic from hearing the dying cries of the other horse.

Stone, stepping close, grabbed the reins of Nibbs' horse and held on. "Get off," he yelled.

Nibbs, the last one to be holding a torch, swung it at the dark gunman. Jack Stone pulled a pistol then and moving in shoved it into Nibbs' belly and pulled the trigger. The old cowpoke let out a squeal like a slaughtered hog and fell back. Stone pushed him to the ground and leapt into the saddle. Laying low he fought to turn the horse, still wild with fright, and managed, in spite of continued volleys of gunfire, to gallop off in the opposite direction from which he had come, riding west into a darkening night.

Quinn had searched the dead man's pockets and found his

wallet. It contained only two paper dollars and some cattle receipts for cows he'd sold for Starkweather. Digging deeper into a compartment he found a wrinkled photograph of a girl. It looked like it had been in his wallet for many years, its corners damp with the sweat of many saddle miles. He held it under the moonlight and looked at it. A fold had divided her face, so Quinn could not tell if she was pretty or not. But, she was a gal. It could have been a sister. Or a whore. It could have been anyone. But still, it was a gal.

Quinn put the dollars and the photograph back in the wallet and put the wallet back in the foreman's pocket. He decided to leave Ethan Moss where he was. He pulled Moss's saddle from his horse, then took the saddle blanket and laid it over the dead man then weighted down the corners of it with several rocks, making a temporary grave until he could come back.

Once, he thought he heard gunfire in the far distance and wondered if it was Stone and the raiders. But it was too faint to know. It might just be the noise of the earth as it rebelled against the coming of winter.

With caution they came into the yard, first Marshal Crowe, then Lacrosse, and finally Ernest and August Tundel. They found the man Lacrosse had shot still slumped in his saddle, his horse standing with queer eyes and laid back ears. But the man was dead. He was pulled and laid with arms at his side. Rud found his hat and placed it over his face.

Nibbs was dragged to where this first man was and laid beside him. Soon the other two were there also, making a woodpile of bodies. They would have to wait until daylight before they could know more about each of them.

Lucy came from the house then and stood close to August. She whispered softly, asking him if he was all right. He looked at her and gave her a sober nod. After that they all stood in speechless wonder. They had just killed the core of Starkweather's raiders. For Tundel, bloody as it was, it was the first victory he had had.

Jack Stone made a wide loop and then headed back to report to Starkweather. In one short day everything had gone to hell. He tried franticly to think where Tundel had found such firepower. It wasn't the townsfolk. He left them all snuggled in their fear. All except the blacksmith. He had showed unusual sand, facing a hothead like Quinn like he did. But he had that kid to watch over. It wasn't likely he'd get mixed up in Tundel's fight. And it wouldn't have been Ashmun. He wanted Tundel gone too.

Then Stone remembered Ike Werth. Starkweather had asked him where that marshal was now, and Ike said he figured he was still at Fort Tillman. But he didn't say for sure. Maybe that old lawman came back. Maybe that ambush tonight was his doings. Stone remembered Starkweather talking about the war and how that old buzzard was crafty as a weasel. Crafty or not, Starkweather was down five men now. Six, counting Milo Clemons, who got himself killed in Fort Tillman. And then there was Clint, at the ranch. And the two murdered cowboys up at the Melgoza range. That makes nine.

Nine men dead in a few days, Stone thought. And then there was Blake, turning traitor. It was starting to seem unprofitable to be working for Starkweather. Something would have to be done.

Starkweather had lanterns burning in every room of the big house. And he had spent time in each room during the long night, pacing and planning. The riders on the Tundel raid were overdue. It was nearing three in the morning and still no word. From one room to the next he paced, calculating his next move, which would be against Ashmun. And then, the range would be his. He knew that Ashmun had a contract with the army to deliver beeves in the spring, but with Ashmun out of the way, the contract would be his.

From an upstairs window he saw a shadow cross the moonlit horizon, a horseman, riding down into the ranch. Scrambling down the stairs he went straight to the porch just in time to see Jack Stone gallop his lathered horse into the yard. Except it wasn't Stone's paint, it was the black Nibbs always rode.

"What's going on," he hollered as Stone left the saddle.

Stone tried to gain his composure. "The worst news." He looked around then, expecting to see Quinn and Moss' horses. "Where are they?"

"Who?

"Quinn and Moss."

"Why would they be here," Starkweather asked.

"Moss is all shot up. Probably dead by now. Quinn was supposed to bring him in."

"Dead. Talk man. What happened? Who killed him?"

"Ashmun's foreman killed him. In town."

Starkweather saw a spittoon setting on the corner of the porch and he kicked it, sending it flying across the yard with a bounce.

"It's worse than that, Douglas. Tundel laid an ambush for us. I'm the only one got out."

This was more than Starkweather could handle. Boiling with fury he headed straight for Jack Stone, needing someone to punish. But Stone met him with two drawn pistols and Starkweather froze. "That won't do," Stone said coolly. "I'm not one of your whipping boys."

They stood apart for a while, and then Starkweather turned and stomped back to the porch. Stone spoke to him in a flat voice. "It's unraveling, Douglas. You're taking too many losses."

Starkweather turned back, his rage still there. "You sound like Lee now. Giving up the cause. Stonewall would never have quit. If he'd lived."

"That is the point, Captain," Stone said mockingly, his pistols still drawn. "Not that many of your boys are still living either."

Another pause.

"I never took you for a quitter, Jack."

"I'm not a quitter. I just know when it's time to get out. And now's the time."

"You and Shelby. When the gold's gone. When the power's gone. You go back to old Union ways. You are a disgrace."

Jack Stone holstered his pistols and stared at Starkweather with a contemptible grin. "Don't bother paying me, Douglas. I'll just help myself to a fresh horse and we'll call it even."

Starkweather gave no reply, just went inside and waited for dawn.

For Tee Blake, morning couldn't come fast enough. The night had been long and he hadn't slept a wink. Sitting on the corner of a horse trough, he watched the sky turn a wintry pink in the east. A cold wind had come up in the night and snow seemed poised in the mountains, waiting for a day just like this. Huddled in a heavy coat, he tried halfheartedly to roll a cigarette but the wind blew the tobacco away and so he gave up. He heard the back door to the kitchen open and saw the flash of a skirt. It was Yuridia, gathering sticks from the wood box for the stove.

She was why he could not sleep. Sitting with her behind the granary yesterday in Dry Branch while the others took the wagon in, had left him feeling awkward and uncomfortable. Neither spoke a word for nearly ten minutes. When he finally built up the nerve to ask her if she was okay, did she need anything, a blanket to keep her warm—even though he had none to offer her—she answered with a voice so soft it reminded him of the tall prairie grass when the wind is up.

She looked at him twice. Once then, when he asked if she needed anything. And right at the end, after Bridges had shot Moss. She turned her eyes to him with a strange terror, as if at that moment she really did need something. Lacking any understanding of what women needed, he only returned her look. It wasn't until later, in the quiet of the ranch yard, after all the lights in the house were out, that he wondered if maybe she didn't need his arms around her. But what did he know, foolish as he was.

Brady Quinn had scanned in all directions making sure Ashmun didn't have any riders nearby. He was a good mile from the house but he saw cattle bunched along the western draw, out of the wind, eating at any tall grass they could find. Most riders would be huddled around a campfire now, drinking coffee and keeping warm. The cattle were content as honeybees.

But riding straight in would never do. He might have to wait until nightfall again. But if he could just get close to Freya Ashmun he might be able to take her for his own. He didn't want to hurt her. Not like Jack Stone. But a little tap on the head might keep her from screaming. Then he could throw her over his saddle and they could ride all night. If they made it to Fort Tillman they could catch a train to St. Louis. Or maybe they'd just keep riding north, toward Billings.

After a half hour of lying in the grass, he decided to get closer. He rode slowly, concealing himself behind the rim of a hummock that bordered the ranch. On the lee side of a cluster of sagebrush he could see directly down into the yard—the corrals, the house, the bunkhouse and the barn. They made a neat little package, he thought.

There was smoke coming from the kitchen chimney and after a while Quinn saw the front door open and three men walk out onto the veranda. He knew one of them immediately as Tee Blake. The other two were Ashmun himself, and Wes Bridges, the foreman. Quinn watched them as they tramped the grounds, each taking his turn talking. Finally the old man motioned toward the barn and all three of them entered through the big door. Five minutes later the three men rode out of the barn and headed in the direction of where the cattle were grazing.

Brady Quinn could not believe his luck. He was in his saddle in a flash and riding down into the yard. He sat his horse beside the corrals for a long minute to see if anyone else stirred, and if they did, he would shoot them. Tying his horse to a rail, he strode confidently to the veranda and knocked on the front door. Like taking candy from a baby, he thought.

The door opened, but it was not Freya Ashmun, it was a Mexican girl.

"What ezz it you want?"

"Who is it, Yuridia?" Freya called from the other room.

Quinn pushed Yuridia aside but she pushed back, and then screamed. Freya came running and when she saw that it was Brady Quinn she looked around for something to hit him with. Finding nothing she flew at him, her little fists flailing. With the back of his hand he knocked Yuridia to the floor, and then turning to Freya, he grabbed her by the arm and wrenched her close to him.

"Get out," she screamed.

Quinn grabbed her hair and held her head back. "I just want a kiss, girl."

She spit in his face. Enraged, he started dragging her toward the door by her hair.

"My father will kill you."

"Yer daddy ain't here. You'll calm down in a minute."

She screamed again and when he tried to get her through the door she braced her feet against the jambs and locked her knees.

"Stop being so difficult." He yanked her to her feet, threw her over his shoulder and marched out into the yard. She pounded on his back and tried to kick him with her knees but he held her tight.

"I'm goin to set you on my horse now. Stop fightin or I'll have to knock you out." He set her on her feet and turned her around. He wanted that kiss he craved. He wanted it now, so he forced his face into hers but just as his lips touched hers she bit him as hard as she could.

Brady Quinn pulled back in pain, his lip giving off a

shower of blood, and as he did, Freya broke loose and ran as fast as she could to the barn. Wiping at his mouth, he watched her disappear into the gloom and rushed in after her.

Swallowed by the shadows, he hollered. "Where are you?"

He listened to the hollow silence, the smell of straw and horseflesh strong in the big dim room.

"We need to get out of here before they come back."

He studied the labyrinth of stalls; saw saddles stacked on wooden frames and bridles hanging from nails. Through a side window he could see dust floating in the air, and the cooing of mourning doves in the rafters. He moved forward, under the fluttering of wings, and then stopped, straining to listen. He thought he heard breathing, behind a wooden barrier. He moved toward it and Freya stepped out from behind it, a four-pronged pitchfork in her hands. With one desperate thrust she drove it into his middle. It went in easy and lodged squarely in his stomach and then she pushed again, forcing it deeper.

Astonished, Brady Quinn staggered back, choking out a groan.

Freya held on to the pitchfork tightly. Blood had begun seeping out of the puncture wounds now and he was making a feeble effort to reach for his pistol. But one of the prongs had penetrated his wrist making his arm immobile. Their eyes locked.

"This is too good for you," she cried. Quinn was bucking against the pitchfork, but she held it fast, like a lasso on a wild horse.

Suddenly, Yuridia came through the big door. Clutched in both hands was a long, sinister-looking Colt dragoon. Her face carried the beginning of a bruise from where she had been slapped, and the dark beauty of her face, mixed with the tangle of her raven hair, made her seem like the very Angel of Death.

Without a word, and without hesitation, Yuridia put the pistol barrel to Brady Quinn's forehead and pulled the trigger.

Chapter 9

WHEN ASHMUN, BRIDGES, and Blake descended the hill into the Tundel yard they were surprised to see four dead men being pitched into a single open grave. The two lawmen, Tundel and August acknowledged them; shovels in hands, hatless, with sweat glossing their brows. Ashmun swept his eyes across the scene, attempting to calculate the full measure of what had taken place. Blake climbed down out of his saddle and taking the shovel from Tundel helped August fill in the hole.

"You missed the great battle," Lacrosse said, managing a smile.

"It appears so," Ashmun said. "But it doesn't look like I was needed."

"There's more to be done," the deputy said. "It's been a killing time. But it's not over yet."

"Is Starkweather among that bunch," Ashmun asked, tilting his head towards the grave.

Crowe shook his head.

"Well, I'm here to add flour to the gravy," Ashmun said. "I see you butchered that steer that you shot in the stampede."

"Done it yesterday," August said, without losing his place in his shoveling.

"What'd you do with the hide?"

"It's hanging on the other side of the barn, curing," he replied.

"I'd like to take a look at it, if you don't mind. Blake, I need you to look too."

All shoveling ceased then as each of the men walked to the side of the barn and examined the tawny steer skin.

"Right there," Blake said, pointing. "You can see where a running iron was used to change the Ashmun A brand to Starkweather's inverted diamond."

Every man took his turn looking closely.

"I never saw it done myself, but I heard Starkweather give the order to the range riders," Blake said.

"On top of everything else," Ashmun said, "he's a rustler too."

Boone Crowe, who had been silent throughout, stroked his mustache with a gloved hand. "If I arrest him will you testify in a court of law, Blake?"

"I will," he said.

"What about my murdered sons?" Tundel added.

Crowe frowned. "These are strange times in Wyoming, Mr. Tundel. In many courts, killing men comes after stealing cows. I don't agree with that. I don't even understand it. But I've seen it done that way."

"He'll get the rope, either way," Lacrosse said.

Tundel's sorrow was like a craggy, battered map upon his face, all his recent losses etched there.

Boone turned to his deputy. "Let's saddle up, Rud. I'd like to get this over with."

"We'll go with you," Ashmun said. "It won't hurt to have added numbers."

They moved towards their horses.

"I'll be riding along," Tundel said.

"That won't be necessary. You've done a brave thing by fighting already."

Tundel's voice carried a sharp edge. "I got a right, marshal. If he hangs, I'll be there for that too. But I deserve to see the look on his face…when…if…"

"You're right. You are right about that. Come along then."

Douglas Starkweather was in the big barn, just throwing a saddle on his horse when the old cowpuncher Tally rushed in.

"There's riders' comin in, boss." Tally's face still showed the marks of Starkweather's fury two days before.

"How many?"

"Five. Maybe six. Comin from the west."

"They our boys?"

"Couldn't tell," Tally said, though he knew perfectly well they were not.

Starkweather hesitated, his hands on the cinch. Through the open air of the barn he could hear the approaching rumble of hooves. "Here. Finish this up. Have him ready to ride in case I need him in a hurry." Then he turned and walked through the barn door, hurrying towards the house. He was halfway there when Boone Crowe and the others rode in and cut him off.

Dust from the horses swept across the yard and

everything seemed to settle into an eerie stillness. "Don't rush off, Douglas," Crowe said.

Starkweather turned and faced them. "You're on my land again, Boone. Only this time you're not welcome. You either, Ashmun."

"We've had to move a lot of dirt today because of you," Crowe said. "Buried four of your men this morning. And Ike Werth yesterday."

Starkweather stiffened.

"Your game's played out. I'm here to arrest you."

"Arrest, hell," he said. Pulling his pistol he made a wild dash for his porch, firing two shots as he ran.

Crowe's party whirled, scattering, but Rud Lacrosse, his pistol already out, leveled a returning shot, hitting Starkweather in the leg. Starkweather fell but still firing continued limping towards his front door. He crashed through it and kicked it shut behind him before a volley of bullets tore at it, leaving flecks of flying oak.

Everyone was off his horse now and Blake, the ever-alert cowboy, grabbed the reins and hustled them into a holding corral, and then, further, into the barn. Once inside he saw Tally standing in the shadows. Blake pulled his pistol and sized up the old wrangler.

"You won't be needin that, Tee. I got no beef with you."

Outside they could hear random gunshots. Blake kept him covered.

"I heard ya jumped, Tee. That was a smart thing. Least ways you might be dead with the rest of em."

"Where's Stone?"

"He lit out. Early this mornin."

"Where was he off to?"

"Didn't say. But I reckon you won't be seein him again. He's a killer but he ain't a gambler."

Blake moved closer. "What're you here for. And what happened to your face."

"Starkweather. Had one of his spells."

"Where's the rest of the riders?"

"There's only bout four left and they's with the herd."

They both listened to more sporadic gunfire. "What's goin on out there?" Tally asked.

"Marshal come to arrest Starkweather. I reckon this could be his last day." He looked to see how this registered with Tally.

"The sooner the better suits me," the wrangler said, nodding.

"Fine then," Blake said. "Why don't you sit down on that milk stool there and don't cause no mischief. And while you're waitin you might as well unsaddle that horse. Starkweather won't be needing it today."

Outside, the standoff continued. Starkweather, armed with a rifle now, had moved to the second floor and was firing from a window, his bullets tearing at corral posts and watering troughs but hitting no one. After a while he would move to another window and repeat the action. No man spoke; the only sound was the steady crack of gunfire.

Far to the left, Ernest Tundel braced himself behind a pile of split wood. He had been scanning the house trying to determine which window Starkweather might fire from next, hoping to get a scoring shot. But then, as he scrutinized the third floor windows, he saw, reflected in the glass, what looked like a lantern's glow. He had with him the Sharps .44-90 that Virgil had done his work with and which Little George had tearfully returned to him.

Adjusting himself against the woodpile, he rested the old Buffalo gun on a sturdy log and aimed for the glowing window. The rifle roared and with the shattering glass came a flash of sparks. The Sharps made such a racket that all other heads turned in Tundel's direction. Within minutes, smoke began to billow out of the upper room, followed a few moments later by flames. Starkweather's house was on fire.

Now they simply watched and waited. The wood was dry and burned quickly and before long the entire house was wearing a crown of flames, working its way downward. Black smoke threw a blanket over the sun giving the entire yard a surreal amber glow and they watched as the smoke shouldered off into the hills.

"Come out," Crowe hollered, but Starkweather answered with more wild shots.

"Ashmun's watching the back," Lacrosse said. "He'll have to come out one end or the other."

Timbers were falling now, toppling into the yard, sparks cascading wildly into the blackening air, the entire second floor a raging inferno. Then, with a thundering groan, one whole side of the main floor began to disintegrate, and the entire structure seemed to blow out a surrendering whoosh of dying breath.

Suddenly, in the very middle of this collapse, the front door opened and onto the porch and down the steps raced Douglas Starkweather, his entire body engulfed in flames. He rushed, a consumed fireball, across the yard, a wild, final Rebel yell cutting the shocked heavens. When he finally fell, still burning, the scream died with him.

The heat from the house was unbearable now and Boone and his posse moved back, the blaze reddening their faces. They stood in wonderment, staring at the smoldering heap that was all that remained of Starkweather. Finally Lacrosse dipped a bucket into the horse trough and threw it over the dead man, sending up a gush of ashy smoke and the horrible stench of burned flesh.

The fire and smoke had lifted alarm with the herd riders and they came thundering over the hills and into the yard, their faces showing shock and confusion, but none of them raised a fight. They did not understand at first that the pile of ashes lying in the yard was their boss. When they did realize, they turned to Tally, who was standing in the yard with the rest of them.

"Whose watchin them critters if'n you're all down here?" Tally barked.

The riders sat their horses and stared. Then, without a word, they reversed their course and rode back to the herd.

Boone Crowe went to Tundel and spoke softly. "It may never be enough. But at least you know it was you that brought him to this."

Tundel nodded gravely.

"Now why don't you go on back home."

Ward Ashmun, Bridges, and Blake caught up with their own men and the herd and told them what had happened to Starkweather. No tears were shed over this news. They had grown to despise Starkweather and his outfit, reinforced over the last week by some of Blake's telling encounters working for the crooked rancher.

It was dusk when they finally reached the ranch house. They found Freya and Yuridia sitting side-by-side on the porch, the horror of their violent morning having settled finally into its own grim reality, though the color that had drained from their faces hours before had not yet fully returned. The old dragoon that Yuridia had taken from Ashmun's desk drawer was still lying on the porch boards beside them.

"What's this," Ashmun asked, dismounting. "You call this a welcoming committee?"

"What…what happened to your face, girl?" Blake asked suddenly, looking at Yuridia, one side of her face fully bruised.

Freya's anger over having been left alone was long gone. They had met their danger together and conquered it. Neither girl spoke now; they simply led the party of men into the barn where Brady Quinn lay, the pitchfork still protruding from his middle. A gruesome furrow bore the upper half of his head away into a bloody mess, where barn rats had already been at work.

Bridges pulled the pitchfork out of the young killer and stabbed it into a pile of hay. "Tundel will want to know about this," he said. "I'll ride over in the morning and tell him."

"There's kerosene over in the tack room," Ashmun said. "He doesn't deserve anything better than what Starkweather got. I don't want his stinking flesh put in my ground."

Bridges and Blake exchanged glances, then unquestioning, set about the gruesome task.

Hours later, after a bland supper that no one could get interested in, and after all events of the day had been told and retold, Tee Blake excused himself and went outside. It was cold and the dark, starless sky was hanging low. He circled the house and stood outside the back kitchen door. He could hear Yuridia attending to the supper dishes, and standing in the dark, peered through the window at her.

Even with a battered face, she's lovely, he thought.

After a long time the Mexican girl opened the kitchen door and pitched the dishwater out onto the yard. When she saw Blake standing there in the shadows, she started.

"It's only me."

"What are yooy doing out here?"

"I…I was hopin to see you."

"But Señor Tee, yooy saw me at de table."

"I know. I wanted to see you alone."

She set the washbasin down. "Why you want to see me?"

Blake let out a deep sigh. "I wanted…to say that I'm awful sorry for what happened. If I had been here…" His words trailed off.

She left the porch and came to where he was standing.

"I mean…I'm sorry about this," he said, his hand moving slowly to her face. His fingers were cold but they felt good against her hot face. "But it doesn't change how you look. Least ways not to me. It'll heal."

She gave him a puzzled look.

"I mean. What I mean is…I…I think you are the prettiest thing I've ever seen."

They stood this way, looking into each other's faces for a long, wordless moment. Then, with more reckless courage then he ever knew he possessed, he leaned towards her and kissed her on the lips. She did not move until he kissed her again. Then she moved in close and wrapped her arms around him.

Walking Fox Carter, his long beard flecked with streaks of gray, rode one mule while holding the lead rope of another. His buckskin leggings and vest were bleached nearly white from a half-dozen summers in the Bitterroots, with head covering made from the skin of a wildcat, Carter was the last of a departed breed. Fur trapping as a profitable industry was long dead, but Walking Fox Carter still kept to the wilds because he fancied the old lifestyle. He had his little niches and hideaways up in the hills where he was not pestered and was able to get by on what he shot or trapped for food. With Indians no longer around to harass him much, life was quiet.

Too quiet.

After leaving Fort Tillman months ago, he sought out an old lean-to he had built years before and planned to enjoy the fall and winter storing up a supply of fish and venison, then sleep through the dark months. Afterward he might canoe down some forgotten river to a peaceable Indian camp and gamble with the natives. But bad luck befell him when he unearthed an old beaver trap and the spring jaws, still set, tore into one of his ankles, nearly cutting it in two. Using all his doctoring skills, learned in the mountains from both Indians and some of the fading old trappers, he sewed and stitched and medicated with herbs the damaged foot. But for two long months he remained immobile, nearly starving to death.

He used that time to brood about the old days. He missed the hunt. He missed the teeming wildlife. He even missed the fear of being stalked by the nasty Blackfeet. In the old days he didn't need more than the company of the ravens and squirrels. He enjoyed sitting over his pot of boiling stew, adding wild ingredients as he saw fit. He remembered the time he was pinned down for three days by a band of trouble-making Crow, back before they took a liking to the white man, helping to scout their enemies. It seemed like good fun for the little group of young Crows, but he recalled it being a fight for his life. Either way, he missed it now.

When the first snow started to fall through the leaky roof of his lean-to, Walking Fox Carter decided he might want to winter in the unaccustomed company of fellow humans. So he hobbled to his mules, took what he couldn't bear leaving behind—rusty kettles, handmade spears and sooty lanterns—and headed back to the strange world of civilization. He arrived in Dry Branch one day after Marshal Boone Crowe and Deputy Rud Lacrosse came to town to buy a bath and a shave.

The whole town watched the old trapper meander down the wide street pulling his mule and listening to the rattle of his pots and pans, banging out a merry symphony. Young Tanner Hornfisher watched with delight at the animal-skinned man nodding half-asleep in the saddle. The two lawmen, enjoying cigars inside Leyland's saloon, themselves all washed and polished, watched through the window.

It seemed to take forever for the mountain man to climb down from his mule and tie up his rig to the hitching rail. The mules drank deeply from the ice-crusted trough and Carter, blinking at his surroundings like a mole, brushed at his beard and then limped into the saloon. The smell of camp sweat and grisly living entered with him, filling the room with an unasked-for bouquet of smoky wildness.

"What'll you have?" Leyland asked, squinting back pungent tears.

"Beer. How's that?"

"Beer I have. Cold even," Leyland said. "And I've got a bath house in the rear too, if you're so inclined," he added boldly.

"I'll get to that." Carter laughed a squeaky laugh. "I et a skunk a week back. They linger some."

It had been three days since the fiery affair at Starkweather's ranch. It had snowed again and this time it stuck. But Crowe and Lacrosse relished the calmer days, where there had been no further killing. The two lawmen had escorted Tundel back to his farm, offering encouragement about the days ahead. *There'll be a lot to sort out in the coming months,* Crowe told him. *But I think the big threat to you and your family is over.* Then he and Lacrosse headed into Dry Branch to hash over their own individual futures. Now, watching the smelly old frontiersman tinker with his money pouch to find a piece of silver for his beer, a sudden thought came to Boone Crowe.

Forgetting the stench, Crowe came to his feet and settled in at the bar. "Mister," he said. "You are a rare creature in these parts. Have you ever run across a trapper by the name of Walking Fox Carter?"

"Well, now," the mountain man squeaked, pulling at his beard. "I's heard that name abouts. Fact, most of my life I've heard it. Some folks say Walkin Fox Carter. Others Louis Carter. Some others Cottonwood Carter. But mostly it's been Walkin Fox. What's yer interest?"

"I'm looking for him."

The trapper let out a loud, joyous roar. "Wall, you sure done come on him. I'd be that feller myself."

This revelation jolted the lawman. It had been Deacon John's words, telling about Eva, how he hadn't seen who it was had picked her up at the train depot, but that Carter was there and may have seen who it was. The marshal's hands took up a mild trembling. "Mr. Carter. I'd like to ask you a question or two."

The old trapper saw Boone's badge and his eyes narrowed. "I ain't in no trouble am I?"

"No. No, I want to ask you about something you might have seen. Several months back. In Fort Tillman." The words seemed to flood out of him and he watched as the old man tried to keep up.

"I surely remember that day. I'd jist guided them army boys on an old Injun path. They was lookin for something and I can't tell you what cause I don't remember. Took em down into Utah country and back. But I 'member the day you speak of. I 'member cause I came upon that same family and their wagon on the trail. They was headin to their farm and I was headin into the hills."

"Who were they?" Boone asked slowly, trying to control his emotions.

"Wall, I knew I'd never forget. Since I spint mosta my life livin in the woods. That was their name. It started with wood. Turns out it was—"

"Woodson," Crowe blurted.

"Thet was it. You got it right. Wood-Son."

Lacrosse was up now too and he saw that Boone Crowe seemed unsteady on his feet. Putting his hand on the marshal's elbow, he guided him away from the bar and back to their table.

Everything around Crowe became a tomb to him. All he could hear was the hollow echo of the Woodson's bare, lifeless yard, and the strange uneasiness—near deadly fear—that gripped him when he wanted to enter the half-burned house.

"Did I say somethin wrong?" Carter asked.

Lacrosse shook his head. "He'll be fine. Just a start."

After a minute, Clive Leyland came to their table with a glass of water. He sat down and pushed the glass slowly across to the marshal, who was sitting with pallid face and remote eyes. Crowe pulled his hat off and laid it on the table, then picked up the water and drank it down. Sweat had come out on his forehead and he wiped at it with his bare hand.

Leyland leaned in. "I'm trying to put some things together here. Something that happened about that same time. About the time Woodson got burned out. I never thought about it before. Until now. Now I have to ask myself—"

"Spit it out," Lacrosse said.

"Well, maybe you ought to talk to the smithy. It's about that old Indian fellow he's keeps out back. The blind one."

Matthew Hornfisher sat on a wooden crate, leather apron across his lap, his hands fidgeting absently with a worn-thin horseshoe.

"I found him stumbling around in circles out in the grassland. He was half crazy and covered with blood. A real mess. Eyes cut out. Tongue cut out. Who wouldn't be crazy?"

"So, there was no way of knowing what happened,"

Crowe said.

"Some Indians are famous self-mutilators. But this wasn't anything like that. This seemed like a vengeance play. Plain hateful cruelty."

"How is he now?"

"He can still be wild sometimes. Certain things will set him off. It's my boy who looks out for him. Tanner's done good to win his trust."

"How far was this from the Woodson place?"

"Southeast of there, following that little creek. About half a mile."

Boone Crowe moved to the wide door of the shop and stared across the street. Even the snow did not keep the Indian from following the guide rope between his little shack and the hog pens. He still looked every bit the Indian, a heavy robe of calfskin draped over his shoulders, hair braided, a wounded nobility etched into his face. Even the dark, empty eye sockets did not diminish this.

"I was looking for a woman. A lady friend," Crowe said, without turning around. "I fear she is dead. So now…now I am looking for where she might by lying. And whoever it was who ended her life."

These were hard words and Matthew Hornfisher was no stranger to their pain. He continued to toy with the horseshoe. "You think my Indian might know something, don't you."

"I doubt if he's the one who harmed her. You don't believe that either. Otherwise you'd never let your boy near him. No, but he might have seen who did. And that would explain a lot about what happened to him."

"You want to try and talk to him, don't you?"

Crowe finally turned and faced him. "Did you see that mountain man hobble in here a while ago?

Matthew nodded.

"I think that old trapper is about half Indian himself. I'd like to see if they could communicate someway."

"I'll get my boy. He'll need to be there to keep the Indian steady."

At Walking Fox Carter's suggestion, an old buffalo robe was laid outside on the snow so he and the Indian could hold council in the open air, cold as it was. The trapper had been delighted at the chance to talk to Coyote, and even though it would be solemn information they were seeking, it would be an opportunity for him to test his skills.

Coyote, perhaps reassured by the many familiar and wild scents that hovered around Carter, came to the buffalo robe with relative calm. Tanner was there holding on to his arm, helping him, as there was no rope to guide him. They sat down and with a gentleness that seemed unusual for the hardy mountaineer, he reached out and took the hands of the Indian. They remained that way for a full minute, communicating, through some unexplained medium, a primitive trust.

Crowe, Lacrosse, and Matthew Hornfisher stood back, out of the circle. Boone had briefed Carter earlier about what he hoped to learn. How he did it was up to him. So when Coyote allowed his spread palms to enclose Carter's hands, and when Carter began to move his own hands in smooth butterfly gestures, the Indian's face brightened. Over the next ten minutes they exchanged gestures in this manner, Coyote sometimes getting very animated, sometimes showing deep expression across his sightless face. At one point he reached out and touched Carter's neck and let his hand flutter into the empty air like smoke, then quickly returned to their joined hands, his fingers moving in what seemed a wordless poetry. Again, the Indian's hand went to Carter's face, and with a single finger touched a place on his upper cheekbone, gently pushing, as if to indicate a mark.

Carter turned and looked at the marshal and nodded faintly, then did the same to Tanner, who touched the Indian lovingly, indicating the interview was over. The party broke up and Coyote was returned to his shack. Carter stood and lifted the buffalo robe, shook the snow from it, and folded it into a square. Marshal Crowe stood by patiently, trying to prepare himself for what he knew might follow.

"It was as you guessed, marshal," Carter said. "This here's a nephew of Looking Glass, that old dead Nez Perce chief. Probably had a hun'red nephews. I din't ask what he was doin wanderin around here. But he saw what you feared he saw alright. And it weren't pretty, I am sorry to report. It was jist turning dawn. Saw the woman on the run. The man who kilt her right after. The man used this here Injun's own knife to cut out his eyes."

Boone Crowe stood in rigid silence, listening. Finally

Carter told him what he'd waited to hear.

"Wore two guns," Carter said, slapping both hips. "Had himself a star-shaped scar up here on his cheek. And a bandana the color of the sun. Yeller, I reckon."

"Jack Stone," Lacrosse said.

"Where is she," Crowe asked, voice unsteady.

"Wall, here's where this Injun showed grit. Even after, bleedin half to death, he found the woman. She was dead. So, figurin he was dead too, he scraped out a grave fer her."

"Where is she?"

"Up by that creek. He called it 'dead woman creek'."

Marshal Crowe's shoulders lifted and his chest rose, his whole body seeming to increase in size, and he stood like a bull, the gray sky at his back.

Walking Fox Carter scratched at his beard and shook his head. "He said he still hears her screams."

Hunter crossed the plains at a full gallop. The horse sensed the urgency and gave it all he had. When they reached the Woodson farm, Crowe guided the horse along the creek and followed it southward. It was a small creek but the snow had made it run and after a while it widened and within three-quarters of a mile, it passed through a grove of cottonwoods. It had begun to rain, turning the snow to slush, and putting a slick, wet coat on Hunter, so he moved the horse under the trees and gave him a few hasty brushes with his gloved hand.

The shallow grave was not difficult to find. The Indian had done well with just his hands, but the rough mound showed the signs of unrest. Fearfully, he came to his knees and with trembling hands began to uncover the grave. Eva Gist's face, paled by the cold earth, eyes closed, did not reflect peace. Removing his gloves, he tenderly brushed at the caked dirt until her face shown in its full tortured expression. Her mouth was drawn into a reflex of sadness and her hair, which he had for so long admired, was tangled and matted around her head. The stench of death was gone. She only carried now the fragrance of the soil. Leaning forward, haltingly at first, he pressed his lips against her cheek. Then he wept.

They came out in a wagon and carried her body back to Dry Branch. She was buried on cemetery hill, close to the resting place of Dorthea Hornfisher. Without being asked, Rud Lacrosse had ridden all the way to Fort Tillman and fetched the one-armed preacher. Over the grave he spoke of the mystery of life. *This is the message we have heard from Him*, he said, quoting Saint John. *That God is Light, and in Him there is no darkness at all.* And then he said, in his own words—*The tomb of Jesus was found empty. Though Eva Gist's body was found, her soul was not there. It was with her Lord.* And there, bundled against the cold, the small group sang a hymn.

Later, in the livery, Boone Crowe was putting a saddle on Hunter when the preacher came in.

"Deputy Lacrosse said you wanted to see me."

Crowe shoved his rifle into its scabbard and gave a final pull on the chinches. "I'd like you to do me a favor, padre, if you would. You've done a lot already, I know. They were fine words you spoke today. I'll be thinking about them for a long time, I'm sure."

"Your favor?"

"Yeah, well. Up the range here a'ways, there's a family name of Tundel. There's a fellow here in town, young man they call Little George. He can take you out there. This family, these Tundels, they have suffered plenty in the past days. And now the old woman has taken to her bed in grief. I fear she may die there. And I'd hate to see it as she is needed. You'll find them to be nice folks."

"And that's your favor?"

"It is."

The one armed preacher smiled. "And what can I do for you, marshal. For you personally."

Boone Crowe pulled his hat from his head and let his fingers brush through his graying hair. "You can pray for me, padre, I guess. Pray for me. Because I am about to go to war with the devil."

The full force of a Wyoming winter slammed down from the Rockies and swept across the territory with a vengeance. The whole of the land was blanketed in white, with drifts filling the ravines and canyons and sweeping their snowy dust across the plains. The few bison that remained stood their furry humps against the wind, while cattle, bunched in tight herds, scavenged for buried grass where they could find it. The line cowboys rode along fences pulling frozen calves out of the wire, half freezing themselves in this luckless duty. Smoke rose from sod-house chimneys where even milk cows had been herded inside to live out the cold months with the family, huddled in the smoky gloom of their houses, fighting against the cheerless darkness. The wild, scraggy sagebrush seemed the sole survivors.

Marshal Boone Crowe had picked up the trail of Jack Stone in Bradley but the elusive gunman always managed to stay a few days ahead of him. After they had buried Eva Gist, Crowe had sent Lacrosse back to Buffalo to meet with Judge Schaffer. *Tell him everything that happened. And tell him if he wants my badge, he can have it. But I am on a manhunt and I won't be stopped by any two-bit Wyoming legalities. Tell him all that.*

That was two months ago. Now Crowe was holed up in Bighorn Canyon, hunkering in a cave with every blanket he owned wrapped around his shoulders and a small, smokeless fire at his feet. It would be daylight in another hour and if all signs were correct, Jack Stone was huddled in his own cave not a quarter mile away. Hunter, draped with a tarp, was hidden in a cleft of protective rocks below.

Stone knew he was being hunted and the cat and mouse chase had made one wide circle, all the way up to Yellowstone Lake and then back down through the Medicine Bow country, to here, in the carved red rims of the

Bighorns. Boone Crowe had a full beard and he had a wool scarf around the crown of his hat and head to protect his ears. He sat now, letting his hand caress the dark grains of his Winchester's stock. It was loaded, and Crowe's two pistols were also loaded, the one under his coat, and the hogleg at his side.

The dreams of a hunter are deep and filled with doom. Many nights the marshal had come out of these dreams calling out a name—*her* name. He looked at the old photograph in his watch often, cherishing it, hoping it would wipe out the other memory, the memory of how he found her there in the ground. But in these dreams he also saw Jack Stone, and in the terror of this mad chase, he found himself shooting his pistols at the devil's dark face, only to hear him laugh, unaffected by the bullets. These dreams were the worst. But then he would think about the war. Or the burning dash that Starkweather made that last day as he, like Lacrosse had said afterward, *found his hell a couple of minutes early*. But now he realized, alone in his cave, that there was plenty of hell to go around.

The sun was up and they were in the rocks now, the red crags rising above them, woven, it seemed, by God's artistic hand, into a lacework of secluded beauty. Stone was a shadow against these rocks and he was moving higher, picking his way, dipping down and back out of little rocky notches in the rugged terrain. Crowe had taken a long rifle shot at him that fell short but let the killer know that the gap was narrowing and death for one of them—maybe both of them—was closing in. Where ice had remained in the shadowy clefts, the climbing was treacherous. Both men had slipped and fallen repeated times, but they kept at their ascent, stopping only to catch their breath, which gushed about their heads in a feverish fog.

Crowe took another shot with his Winchester and this time the slug threw up flakes of shale close by the fugitive. Stone turned around then and shot back, his own bullet hitting short but throwing its own rock chips. Finally Jack Stone disappeared into a crevice and Crowe had to stop and do some guess work. He was more exposed than he wanted to be, so, swinging wide he followed an angled notch upward until he believed he was near the place where Stone had dissolved into the rocks.

Boone Crowe waited, listening. Nothing. Then a shadow fifty feet to his left sprang out, followed by the roar of Stone's pistols, and Crowe felt himself thrown backwards. A bullet had hit him in the chest and he could feel a burning on his skin. But instinctively, he leveled the Winchester and fired. There was a thud and Stone spun, leaving blood on the rocks behind him. Ducking back into his hiding place, the outlaw let out a call.

"You'll have to do better than that, marshal."

Crowe didn't answer. He felt inside his coat to where he had been hit and pulled out his hidden pistol, the cylinder smashed by the bullet. Feeling deeper he found his only wound was a small flash burn. The pistol had taken the brunt. He felt an odd urge to smile. But now he could hear Stone climbing again. They were close to the top of this rocky bluff and if Stone got there first he could pin Crowe down easily. So the marshal moved to his right and continued to scale the scraggy slope.

It took long minutes before he finally glimpsed the level plateau above him. He raised his head slowly and there, facing away from him, stood Stone, his pistols pointed downward into the crevice he had just arisen from. The killer was standing at the very rim of the plateau. Alongside him was a drop-off. Just as Crowe rose up, Stone, surprised, turned, then stepping back, fired, but his bullets flew well high as he thrust his arms out, his boots grinding then slipping against the loose, frosty lip and with a hollow gasp of shock fell backwards over the cliff.

Boone Crowe lowered himself to his knees and rested against a rock. He pressed his head there, panting deep worn out breaths. He waited for any noise from Stone but heard nothing. Finally he got up and walked cautiously across the flat plain to the rim of the table and peered over the side. Twenty feet down Jack Stone lay on his back, his arms stretched out and his legs twisted in odd directions, like two opposing fence posts. His eyelids fluttered and Crowe could barely make out a weak moan.

Checking the terrain, the marshal found a weather-battered notch that he could creep down until he was standing on the same ledge where Stone lay. He stood over the outlaw for a long time, bitterness so deep it came up through his throat in sickening bile and lodged there.

"I…I can't move."

Crowe said nothing, only studied the cruel, tormented face. His emotions were at flood stage and he didn't know which direction his fiery hatred might take him. The wind, on this high point, was fierce, and it tore at his coat collar. He stared away then, far across the wide land, at its beauty and its terror, and found that it was still there. For months it had disappeared behind his hatred. But now it was coming back and he sucked in the cold air as if it were a new life. It *was* a new life. Then he removed the watch from his pocket and opening it held the picture of Eva Gist close to Jack Stone's face.

"Look at this."

Stone turned his face.

"Look at it," he hissed. "Do you know what this woman meant to me?" He stopped abruptly. He was suddenly very tired. There was nothing left inside of him. He slowly closed the watch and put it back in his vest pocket.

"Shoot…me…Crowe."

He looked again across the snowy range and to the majestic Tetons far beyond. "You'll probably last awhile before the ravens find you. It's pretty cold up here but I doubt you'll freeze till sometime in the night." His voice was even, calm. "But the critters will have found you by then. If not the ravens then the coyotes. Something will."

"Shoot me…*please*. Don't…leave me like this."

"By summer, though, the rattlesnakes will have made a nest in your rib bones." He was still staring off across the land. "I may come back then, just to see that."

"Pleeeasse..."

But the lawman was already making his descent down through the snowy crags, his heart only half-lifted, but still beating.

Months passed. It was late spring, the long Wyoming winter having surrendered its bitter reign. Marshal Boone Crowe passed high above the Tundel place and saw that the fields were plowed and the early wheat was radiating a healthy green shadow upon the earth. He did not stop—did not want to stop—but even from where he crossed over the far hill, he could see that the old woman was out in the yard, throwing washed bedding across the clothesline, the same place he had first seen her the long months ago. He rode quietly around Dry Branch, skirting the town, and guided Hunter up the hill to the cemetery.

Alone on the range, Crowe had collected some purple prairie flowers and he cradled them now as delicately as if they were eggs. Purple. It had always been her favorite color. There were many things that she loved, and had spoken of, that were coming back to the lawman these days. And he was trying hard to lose himself in those tender memories whenever he could.

He dismounted, walked tentatively to Eva Gist's grave and with clumsy care, placed the flowers at the foot of her marker. He knelt there but found that he had no words to speak. Still, he remained there for a long time, watching the tall grass sway in the wind like the waves of some lonesome faraway sea. Putting his open palm on the mound of earth that was her grave, he held it there, as if expecting to feel a heartbeat. When he finally stood up, he turned to see young Tanner Hornfisher standing in polite silence twenty paces away.

Crowe touched his hat in greeting. "Did you know it was me?"

Tanner nodded. "I noticed Hunter first."

They both stood there for a moment then Tanner walked over and took up Hunter's reins and handed them to the marshal.

Crowe put his hand on Tanner's bare head and tousled his hair. "I don't know if I'll be back this way. And just in case I'm not. Well. It would mean a good deal to me if you'd...look after her." He passed his hand over her grave as he said this.

Tanner's eyes moved among the tombstones, first to his mother's, then to Eva's, and then back to the marshal. "I will," he said. "I'll watch over it."

The lawman tightened the cinch on his saddle, put his boot in the stirrup and hoisted himself aboard. He leaned over and extended his hand. The boy took it and they shook. Then with one last appraisal of the town and then the sky, he nudged Hunter and headed north.

It took a long time for the marshal to finally ride out of sight, but Tanner watched him the whole while, until horse and man disappeared over the farthest hill.

Acknowledgements

Weaned on classical western literature—*Shane, The Searchers, The Virginian, Riders of the Purple Sage*—I have worked to give similar literary depth to the characters in *Dead Woman Creek.* Though the actual writing of a book is primarily a solitary endeavor, its more comprehensive creation and production is, in the larger sense, rarely done without a supporting cast. I am deeply in debt to Christopher G. O. Buchmann for his priceless technical support, and to Rachel O. Boruff (Rachel Thornton Photography) for her brilliant work on the cover of *Dead Woman Creek.* And finally, my most sincere gratitude to Jennifer Moorman for loving Boone Crowe enough to help put him in print.

A wealth of encouragement came from two dear friends, Timothy J. Coder (author of *War Without End, Amen*) and Roger Taylor (author of *Viola and the C-Street Boys*). Sons, Matthew and Alex, resided in the cheering section, both persistent encouragers, ushering me into the technical realm of e-literature.

Characters take on a life of their own, and often share the glory of the actual writing, directing their own movements and motives, frequently requiring the writer to give them their own reins. But real people too can lend their inspiration, and for that I give thanks to my father, a tough old cowboy who chased both mustangs and cattle in his rawhide days, and whose 'tight inside punch' laid a few hombres in the dust. Becca Byam supplied a unique frontier loveliness; an actual Tanner provided youthful grit; and to the memory of my late cousin, Daryl, whose gravel-and-shingle stubbornness, along with his off-handed horsemanship, lent itself to several of my characters.

No one deserves more appreciation than my wife, Rebecca, who thought she married a poet, but got a western writer in the bargain. Her support ranks among the priceless.

About the Author

Buck Edwards was born a flatlander, among cattle and horses, and was weaned on classic western literature–Zane Grey, Owen Wister, Alan Lemay, Conrad Richter.

His *Marshal Boone Crowe series* is his attempt at giving western readers both high adventure, peopled with tough men and women, and heroes, not just with grit and heart, but with a soul. Love on the Wyoming plains is not always easy to find, and if it does come, it comes without the window-dressing.

Buck Edwards knows tumbleweeds and nights by the campfire. He knows beans and bacon and the sound of the lonely wind on a flat prairie night. And he knows that he loves to write.

Dead Woman Creek and *Showdown in Bear Grass* are both available for Kindle. Look for *Showdown in Bear Grass* coming to print in Summer, 2014.

96187249R00148

Made in the USA
Columbia, SC
22 May 2018